Sweet Misbehavin'

McKenna Clan Series Book Three

Christine Young

Published by **Rogue Phoenix Press**

ISBN: 978-1-62420-259-9

Credits
Cover Artist: Gemini Judson
Editor: Christie L Kraemer

Prologue

The Time Before Time

"Atantsi, you must hurry, go now. Or it will be for naught." The girl opened the door, peering down the hall then slammed it shut, her hands shaking.

"Phaedra, I cannot. What about you and my people? He will kill them all and you as well if he discovers the truth. I am his betrothed. I cannot break the promise my parents made to him." Fear spilled down her spine. She couldn't, no she wouldn't risk her people.

"He will not. As long as you are alive he will harm no one. So you must go, take these." Jokul's slave handed her two items. "Whatever happens, protect these with your life because they are your life."

"He wants my homeland and will stop at nothing to gain it." Atantsi looked to the window, wishing the brilliant sunshine pouring through the curtain could warm her heart and chase away the terror.

"But he wants you too. When he believes someone is his, he will never let it go. He will do nothing to harm the ones you love." Phaedra's reassurance helped melt some of the ice encompassing her.

"What are these?" Atantsi turned each in her hand studying them. She knew they must possess some magic or Phaedra would not be so serious.

"The crystal you can use to travel through time. Hold it to the light and think about the place and time you wish to see. Be careful though. You should not jump ahead too many years at a time. It is very dangerous. Use this only in emergencies; only when you sense his presence."

"How will I know? I have no special powers. Even if I did, I have no one to teach me." She knew of people in her country who could do things she'd never dreamed of but she was not one of them.

"You do have powers. Your mother and father thought it best if you never learned of them. But they were wrong. Someday you will have to acquire the knowledge, but not today."

"Maybe not. What is this?" Atantsi opened a small book then slammed it shut. Her breath caught in her throat, the meaning all too clear. She swallowed her panic, hoping to learn more. "I didn't know?"

"You are a firestarter but you were never trained because you were sent here. Your people never had the chance to educate you. Without this knowledge, you will not be able to control the fire. Until you read this and try to teach yourself, you must not let your emotions get out of control."

"I don't understand." Atantsi clung to the little book as if it were her lifeline.

Phaedra held Atantsi's hand in hers. "Until a firestarter is trained, anger, agitation, fear, any stress can cause them to accidentally set something in flames."

Atantsi's stomach churned and her body shook. She withdrew her hand and sat down for a moment, trying to regain the courage she knew she would need. "I don't think..."

"Of course you are afraid but you have no other choice." Phaedra clasped her hands around Atantsi's once again. "I want to reassure you but I won't lie to you, I know you will face danger."

"Really? There is no other way?" Atantsi had never thought of herself as strong or courageous.

"He will bury you in ice if you stay. His power and rage is too great and there are times..." Phaedra stiffened. "He is coming. Do you feel the chill in the air? That is how you will know if he is near."

Atantsi stood then hugged her friend, preparing herself to leave and praying for the strength to elude the demon. "I hope you are right and he does not destroy you and my people with his fury."

"Come." Phaedra pulled her to the balcony. "Think. Where do you wish to go? Just keep thinking and holding this in the light."

Atantsi did as bid, placing the crystal in the light and letting the glow surround her. She felt as if she was lifted from the ground and enveloped in a bubble of soft air.

Flower scented breezes swirled and danced around her. Time seemed to stand still. She closed her eyes, resting in the cushion enclosing her and knowing she would need all of her senses.

What future awaited her? Would she live or die or ever see her sweet Phaedra again?

Thoughts of her mother and father swam through her mind and she sent a silent prayer to the heavens and gods above to keep them safe from the rage of Jokul, the ice demon.

For another moment, she saw the ice beneath her then she was on an island cliff dotted with white houses.

Chapter One

Margo's hand shook when she knocked on the door, room 207. Less than a second later it was opened and she peered inside. Music blared and encased in smoke an almost naked man danced on the table amidst cheers, raucous laughing and shouts of "More, Carr, more. Take it all off. We want to see all of you."

"Miss?" the man at the entrance asked. "Can I help you? Do you have an invitation?"

"Margo." She held out a small white card with lettering embossed in gold. "Here."

"We've been waiting for you." He gestured for her to move further inside then he closed the door behind her.

It clanged shut with an ominous sound. At the noise, the man stopped dancing. He gawked at her as if he'd never seen a woman before. Then he grinned. One dimple on the right side of his face formed and his amber colored eyes glittered as he stared at her. The intensity of his gaze had Margo touching her throat to ensure her soul remained within. A tiny chink of the armor surrounding her and a bit of ice melted from her heart. A searing wave of heat ripped through her. Blindsided, she set one hand on the armrest of a sofa to keep her knees from buckling. In the back recesses of her mind, she remembered Phaedra and her warning.

Calm yourself. Don't want to risk another fire.

He stopped dancing as he continued to stare at her. As if in slow motion, he spread his arms and made a three hundred sixty degree turn.

"Got the hots for the new little lady?" A woman at the table laughed. "She is slammin' but you could have me instead."

As if he suddenly realized that not only was he nearly butt naked, but he was showing the entire audience what he wanted, his wayward body seemed to perform for the woman who just walked in the door. He looked at her for another moment, changed his focus to the lady who'd spoken to him, winked then reached for a cloth napkin, tying it around his neck cowboy style.

His rock hard butt undulated when he continued to dance and sway with the music. Margo felt as if he gyrated for her. His biceps bulged and he sported tiny barely visible tattoos she couldn't quite make out. On his right bicep, running the length, there was a golden-black jaguar. When his arm flexed, it seemed the big cat was running.

How long had it been since a man looked at me like that? Perhaps a century or two, and I don't want him. I don't know him. I'm here for the money, nothing else. No emotional involvement. I can't let anyone jeopardize our safety.

He hopped from the table and prowled his way to a chair where a pair of jeans had been draped. He slipped into them and chugged what appeared to be a shot of whiskey before making his way in her direction, holding out his hand. "Carr McKenna at your beck and call." His gravelly voice purred then he winked, grinning as if he owned the world.

She licked her dry lips and accepted the handshake. "Margo." *This is not happening to me. I've never felt anything for a man and I can't let one into my life now. This is just work, nothing else. Good God, girl, get a grip.*

"Margo?" He grinned.

"Just Margo."

"All right, Margo just Margo, would you like something to drink? Beer, wine, something else?" Cat-like he plopped on a chair beside her, one eyebrow rising as if he read her thoughts. "Are you hungry?"

"Beer would be fine and yes I am—hungry." She played with the silverware, trying to figure out the instant attraction to this man.

"Don't go anywhere." He gave her a look that said *or else*. With incredible grace, he rose and strolled toward the bar.

She couldn't move her feet right now without face planting. So it was not likely she'd walk out the door. She closed her eyes as if the tiny movement would slow her heart.

"Thanks." She didn't think he heard her, but he turned and grinned. He was back before she could take a deep breath and calm her jagged nerves. She'd been terrified before she walked in the door, now there were no words to describe her escalating emotions.

He set the glasses on the table and reached to another table to confiscate a bowl of nuts. "You're mine."

Good God, but he didn't really say that, did he? "Maybe for tonight," she told him, trying to act as nonchalant as the man sitting in front of her. "But it will cost." She looked heavenward as if to pray but she'd rejected religion years ago, knowing it did little good at keeping the demons at bay.

"I'll pay anything you want." Carr turned his chair and sat down, resting his arms on the back. "Set the price."

She didn't know what to say. The escort service was up front about their fees. She couldn't name any price, no matter how tempted. If he paid her enough tonight, she might not have to work for a couple of days and she could spend time with her little girl. If he paid her more, she could run again, find a new place where she couldn't be found and damn the escort service. Yet she knew the demon tracking her would always find her and by herself she wasn't strong enough to fight him.

She heaved a small sigh and sipped her beer. When she looked up, she saw amber-green eyes and concern. "I can't do that. You're here. You must know what the service charges."

"I've never used the service. So tell me. What do they charge?" He seemed to question everything.

His chest, still bare, was sweat-sheened. She had the uncanny notion to reach out and touch him. And of all the crazy things, the need to trace the golden-black jaguar tattoo seemed to overcome all rational thought.

She cleared her throat. "One thousand dollars a night and not a penny more. They frown on girls who charge more, actually they fire them."

"You deserve more." He chugged his beer. "Want another one?" He rose and looked as if he couldn't figure out what to do next.

"No thank you." She looked at her still full glass and slanted him a half-hearted smile. The attraction she felt for this man was undeniable. She'd never thought, after her husband passed, there would be room for a man in her life. But her husband had not been who she'd thought he was. They'd never been in love, but they'd needed each other—until that day. The day she wanted to forget but couldn't.

Stop it. Stop right now. You have your little one to think of—her safety as well as yours. There is no man destined for your future. And you don't want one. This man could be a trap. No emotional involvement.

Carr returned with another beer for both of them. While he'd left, she finished off the glass. Her first drink had gone down way too fast. Needing to keep a tight rein on her emotions as well as her drinking; she vowed to stay sane this night.

"Here you go. You told me no, I get it, but still, I thought maybe... You don't have to drink the beer if you don't want it." He set the beverage on the table then retrieved his shirt. Slipping it on, he sat down beside her. His long legs were stretched beneath the table and he rested one arm on a chair next to him.

Her second thoughts about Carr were pure male animal, primal, sensual and sexual.

She wanted the introductions over, yesterday. "I have to be home by five A.M. Just so you know." Her hands shook and her heart raced. Every nerve ending unraveled when she looked at him.

"Whatever time is fine with me." Four fingers drummed on the table in front of him. It seemed he waited for her to take the initiative.

"I don't do weird things." Nerves splintered inside, the hand holding the beer glass shook.

"You don't need to be afraid." Carr held her wrist, which was shaking. "I don't bite and I'm really very nice. I've never done weird so I won't start now."

Her laugh felt stilted and insincere. "What do you do?" Curiosity killed just about everyone in her life and she told herself she shouldn't be so inquisitive. Holding herself back with this man was proving harder than she'd expected. This was her first day on the job and regrets piled higher than the Himalayas, but for her daughter's sake she had to go through with this.

Jobs had been hard to find. She'd worked as a waitress and a store clerk. She was smart, but her qualifications for anything but minimum wage were nonexistent. She'd given up her idea of further education when she married her daughter's father. Only a few months of that rocky relationship had passed when she realized she'd made a horrible mistake and had set herself up for discovery.

While people thought her husband had been killed in a fire in the Colorado Mountains, he'd become a national hero for a short time. But she knew what really happened. So she hid the bitter truth about his death. If this man sitting in front of her learned about what she'd done, he'd run the other way. She was a black widow, had killed her husband, but she'd had no choice when he'd turned on her.

Ending the relationship would have been natural except for the fact he had threatened to kill her and their little girl.

"Pizza?" The waiter held a steaming pie in front of them.

She shot Carr a puzzled grin.

He shrugged. "Thought you might like something to eat. I'm famished." Carr motioned for the waiter to set the food on the table then handed her a napkin. "Barbecued chicken, pepperoni, Canadian bacon and tomato. Hope there's one you like there."

"What's your favorite?" She reached for a slice of the pepperoni. It was thin crust and just the way she liked it. She hadn't eaten anything but a few chips in almost two days and her stomach rumbled.

"Hmm...pepperoni," she said as she chewed then covered her mouth with her hand. "Sorry."

"Don't be." His grin was wide before he bit down on the chicken pizza.

She ate the slice then reached for another. "This is so good." But her stomach had shrunk. The second piece was more than enough to make her feel so full she thought her belly might burst.

"You can take the leftovers home if you want." Carr motioned for a waiter, asking him for foil when the man arrived.

Heat flooded her face, embarrassment that he might have guessed her near poverty situation. "It's all right. I..." but she thought of her little girl and knew Sophie would love the pizza.

"No, I don't want it. Never eat leftovers."

Why did she think he lied? Pizza was best the second time around or the next morning for breakfast.

"You're mine." A harsh voice behind her pierced the air.

A man Margo had never seen before startled her to full alert, yet she was left speechless.

Carr rose to his feet, hands clenched at his sides and jaw rigid. Margo's heart beat hard and fast, her breaths racing in shallow uneven pulses.

"She is not." Carr's words were a low menacing growl. The possessiveness Margo heard in his voice surprised her.

"I bought and paid for her." The man reached into his pocket and brought out a slip of paper he waved in the air. "A bill of sale."

"How much?"

"Wait." Margo held out her hand in a gesture that seemed to hold him off. She closed her eyes, waiting for the control she needed. She didn't want to start anything she couldn't finish peacefully. Carr had taken on the role of protector, but good lord, she didn't need help. This man should pose no threat to her.

But Carr didn't seem to listen to her. He'd reached into his pocket and pulled out his wallet, which he was thumbing through.

"Two thousand," the man said.

"One thousand," Carr countered. "The agency sets the price and they wouldn't allow you to do business with them if they discovered you'd paid too much."

"One thousand five hundred."

Carr tossed ten one hundred dollar bills at the man. "Take it or leave it." He scooped up the wrapped-in-foil pizza then grabbed Margo's hand and started walking.

She scrambled to her feet in an attempt to stay upright and followed. "Carr..."

"What?" he growled, turning to her. "My apologies, I'm not angry with you."

"Accepted." She paused. "Your apologies, but I'm not sure why."

"That man made my blood boil." He turned and slanted her a cheeky grin. "Let's forget him."

"Forgotten." She liked the feel of her hand in his. His was calloused and strong. He hung onto her and the feelings emanating from him into her gave her courage when she'd had all but given up hope.

"Where are we going? I'd rather go to your room." She wasn't sure she was ready for sex with this man or any other, but she'd contracted with the agency and knew it was expected.

"Neither," was his curt reply.

"Then where?" She felt a shiver of ice touch her spine. "I don't know what you're thinking but..."

"Hush, it's nothing kinky. I want to take you out on the lake. A buddy of mine owns a boat shop and he rents out canoes, rowboats, sailboats and whatever appeals."

"Isn't it closed this time of night?"

"I know where the spare key is but I'll give him a quick call so he doesn't send the cops."

"What if we tip over? I'm not sure, I know it's possible in a canoe. I don't want to get wet."

He stopped and she nearly tumbled but caught herself. "Whatever are you thinking? We're going for a romantic stroll on top of wonderfully blue water in a canoe and we won't tip over."

Blood rushed to her cheeks and her nose felt hot. "Oh, ok."

~ * ~

Carr McKenna had never felt so exhilarated. He'd dated and had sex with many women but no one had melted his heart so thoroughly and so quickly as Margo.

The ride to the lake had been slow and quiet. He'd executed the drive with thoughts of what exactly he intended when they arrived at the boathouse. All the while he'd drunk in the lemony scent that emanated around her. With dark brown eyes and amber-colored hair, her ivory skin and delicate features were framed to perfection.

"Here we are." He pulled the car into a parking spot. His chin rested on the steering wheel as he looked at the lake. "The lake's beautiful, takes my breath away every time I look at it."

Moonlight hit the ripples made from the light breeze blowing down from the mountain. This was one of his favorite spots—winter, spring, fall and summer it was spectacular. A couple of times every year, he left Cactus Junction, Nevada and visited, trying to alternate the seasons.

"Now what?"

"I'm calling my friend." He pulled out his cell and made contact. "Hey bud, it's me and I'm at your business. Wanted to rent a canoe."

Margo had turned her head to look at him. He gave her a thumbs up as he nodded to his friend who must have been asking him why. "Want to impress a date," Carr said into his phone.

"Impress me?" One of her eyebrows lifted and she smiled. "I'm not exactly a date."

"Your smile is breathtaking," he whispered to her while listening to his friend. "No I'm not talking about your smile and I do know where to find the key. All right, I will be careful."

He slipped his phone into his pocket then thought better of it and left it below the seat in his car. "We're set to go. Can you swim?"

"Swim? Yes, but not very well. Really, Carr, I don't want to find myself in the lake."

"Do you need to wear a lifejacket?"

"Probably, yes."

A few minutes later, Carr had the garage styled door open and a canoe resting on the slide. He pushed the boat until it sat in the water and handed her the flotation device, which she donned.

"Your water carriage awaits. Do you want a new adventure? If so..." He offered Margo a hand, helping her into the bow. "May I help you?"

"It's tipsy."

"Sit as still as you can and I'll do the rest. No sudden movements." He winked at her.

"Okay boss." She saluted and faced toward the other end of the lake.

"I'm getting in then I'll push off. Do you want to try paddling?" After placing both paddles on the bottom of the boat, he stepped inside, pushing off as he did so.

He heard her soft inhale as the boat glided across the lake where moonlight left a shimmering imprint.

"I'll paddle. It can't be too hard." She turned to reach for the paddle.

Carr showed her how to hold it then placed the paddle in the water and when the stroke was finished, he demonstrated a feathering technique across the surface.

"Good," he told her as he watched her. "Let me know if you get tired."

"So you can have all the fun?" She turned a little too fast, and the boat wavered.

He laughed, loving the little frown he saw on her face. "No, so you can rest if you want." They paddled in silence until they were away from the shoreline.

He set the paddle in the bottom of the canoe. "We're going to float on the water."

"You're tired."

She laughed, and with that he felt a weight lift from his shoulders. He liked to see her smile and hear her laughter. More than anything he wanted to hear real laughter, a laugh that came straight from the belly.

"No. It's so peaceful. I like to listen to the water lap against the side of the boat and watch the moonlight reflect off the surface."

"Tell me about yourself." He wanted to know everything. "Start from the beginning. Where were you born?"

She shrugged, turning from him and seeming to lose focus on their discussion. "Not much to tell."

"Humor me."

He heard her sigh then clear her throat. "I moved here from Colorado a few days ago."

Carr laughed. "Well that's a start, any family?"

"No."

"Do you lie often? Or is it just to me?" He lounged against the back of the canoe, his arms on the gunnels.

She inhaled a swift hiss of air. "It's none of your business."

"About the fib or the family?" For some reason he couldn't fathom, he didn't want to let this go, but he thought he probably should. With time and care he would get to the truth and what she hid from him. Then perhaps he would show her his family secret.

"Both, but I'm not in the habit of lying."

Her tone changed and he sensed anger simmered deep. Changing the subject seemed necessary.

"Have you ever gunneled?"

She shook her head, swiping an errant lock of hair from her eyes. Her brows were drawn together as if she concentrated intensely on something. He smiled.

"I've never been in a canoe before this and I have no idea what you're talking about." She sounded a bit petulant but curious.

"Do you mind if I strip to my briefs?" She'd seen him in his underwear and in the unlikely event he fell in, he wanted to have dry clothes waiting for him.

"Really? Well, I've already seen you dancing. Why not?"

"Come here." He motioned for her to move to the stern of the boat.

"Won't that make this capsize?" She scooted back anyway.

He gave her a quick one-minute lesson on steering the canoe then he stepped on the top of the canoe, placing one foot on each side. "Just sit still and steer."

"What are you going to do?" Panic echoed in each word.

"Watch," he said, not wanting to frighten her. The worst that could happen was he'd end up in the lake. Perhaps a little dip would cool him off. Using his legs and feet, he pushed down on the stern of the canoe, let it come up then pushed again. It began to move forward, picking up speed with each thrust.

"How'm I doin'?"

"Great! Don't fall off."

"I won't." His laughter seemed to echo around the valley.

"Promise?"

"Umph..." He was hit in the gut by a force he had trouble comprehending. Losing his balance and all of his strength, he fell. The lake engulfed him. He struggled to the surface. His body, inside and out, felt iced-over. He reached the top then inhaled a lungful of water as he gasped for air. Fear for Margo swept through him. He'd never been so helpless. Closing his eyes he searched his inner soul for the energy to overcome this horrific cold. Once more he inhaled, and this time sweet air filled his lungs. The canoe drifted aimlessly as he attempted to reach it. His strokes were hesitant at first but as he grew stronger he closed in on the canoe. He raised his head and swam head high, watching the boat and Margo.

She sat slumped over, unmoving, her hair hanging from its pins. She appeared frozen in time. His stomach cramped, yet he fought the pain the blow had inflicted. At the canoe, he pulled himself up and over the gunnel trying not to rock the tiny vessel.

"Margo, are you alright?" He moved her hair back, hoping to see her face but she didn't flinch, didn't change position. Clasping her hands in his, he said, "You need to tell me what just happened here."

She shook her head. "I don't know."

"I think you do but I understand if you don't trust me. Something supernatural just happened and I need to find out what it was so I can fight it." His body shook with the freeze that had engulfed him. Slowly he began to warm.

He dried himself with his shirt and pulled on his jeans then he crouched down in front of her.

She looked up. "You can't know, no one can." Tears slid down her cheeks. "I don't want you in danger."

"I can handle myself," he told her, understanding he couldn't convince her unless he showed her who he really was and he couldn't do that, not yet. If his guess was wrong, he'd terrify her.

"Not against this."

She wasn't going to tell him more and he wanted off the damn lake. For some reason, whatever it was that knocked him in the gut had not found what it was looking for, and he didn't want to take chances while they were vulnerable.

"We need to get to land." Carr picked up a paddle, and to his amazement Margo seemed to come out of her shell. She moved to the bow of the canoe and began to paddle as she sensed the danger too.

It seemed to take a lifetime to reach the boathouse. When the canoe hit dirt, Carr jumped into ankle deep water then lifted Margo from her place in the bow and onto dry land. As quickly as he could, he secured the canoe inside the boathouse then locked it.

"What are you going to do now? I don't want to go back to the condo and it's almost sunrise. The night is finished."

"I'm taking you home." And she was right... The night was finished but he wasn't going to leave her side.

"No." She stood straight and stiff. "I can get myself home."

"How do you plan on getting there?"

"I'll call the service and they'll send a car."

Frustration swept through him. He inhaled a deep breath, trying to remain calm in the face of emanate danger. "I know you don't trust me, don't have a single reason to have faith in me, but I'm the good guy and I'd never hurt you."

"I've heard that before." Her tone sounded jaded, yet too sincere for his liking.

"Come on, just get in the car, please." He didn't want to stand around in the open, and he didn't know what he could do to convince her. "Please."

She stood in place for a few more minutes then seemed to concede. She marched to the car and opened the door. "Take me home then." Arms crossed in front of her, she sat down.

He felt a glimmer of laughter. She was so damn beautiful and this was a first, a tiny opening, a little bit of trust. Perhaps he did knock a chip off her armor. He reached inside to the back seat and pulled out a second set of clothes, dressing quickly.

"I'm happy you agreed. Which way?"

"That way," she pointed. "You always keep an extra set of clothes in your car."

"Always."

Carr pulled up in front of a large brick house on a quiet out-of-the way back street in Tahoe. Drumming his fingers on the steering wheel, he gazed along the road.

"Thanks," she said then stepped from the vehicle.

He leaned toward the open door. "Which house?"

"That's something you don't need to know." She closed the car door and started walking, but he was sure she moved in the opposite direction. Well, two could play this game and he planned to win. He could out last her and if she did lead him to her home all the better. The need to protect her surmounted everything else.

Still watching Margo, he pulled his cell from his pocket and dialed the escort service. A few minutes later, he had booked her for the night ahead of them, and only a few more minutes passed before Margo was sitting beside him again.

"Come back to talk?" He knew she'd not been truthful about her home. She didn't live on this street.

"No, keep driving and I'll show you where I live. Turn left up here."

A little while later, he stopped in front of a small detached home. "This it?"

"Yes." This time she didn't wait. She flew from the car and up the steps to her home, pulling a key from her bag. When she opened the door, an elderly lady waited for her.

He watched as Margo nodded her head and spoke something to the woman who grabbed her coat and purse before leaving.

He leaned back against the seat and took one moment to close his eyes. He woke startled and cursing himself for falling asleep. But when he sat forward and rubbed his eyes, he saw Margo walking from her home with a little girl. *Good God, I would have never guessed, and the woman she was paying was the sitter.*

No wonder she had armor a mile deep, and he had so much to discover about Margo. First, he meant to find out her last name and if this surname was real.

~ * ~

Jokul paced the room, his gut churning with frustration. He looked at the blocks of ice stacked one upon the other, light glimmering off the crystals. He wanted to coat the world in ice right after he found her. He wondered what name she was going by now? She'd make a beautiful ice statue to add to his collection.

He pounded the table holding his glass of merlot—so close but so far away. He'd felt the essence of Atantsi, his betrothed. Had felt her warmth as if she stood beside him, yet he could not find her.

The shapeshifter had received what he had coming to him. He'd thought the shifter would die in the lake but somehow he'd survived. Did the damn cat know anything about Atantsi? No, he didn't think so. The woman in the boat could not have been her.

Where was she? Where was his firestarter?

He couldn't think and he could barely breathe as rage engulfed him and he set frost to shimmer on the earth.

No, he would find her. He always did. Yet this time felt different. She had disappeared without leaving a trace and she'd never been able to do that. Perhaps she'd learned how to mask the heat.

When he found her—and he would—he would make her understand that he ruled her. He would quench her fire.

His fists clenched as he thought on the ice he poured over her homeland when she'd disappeared. All her people, all the people of Angizei ton Ourano, had frozen. They now stood on the cliff as ice statues waiting for her warmth. But the fire she breathed on them would not bring them back to life.

He sat down, knowing the only way he could find her was to calm himself and let his thoughts mingle with those who were thinking of him. And he knew her thoughts were on him. She feared him and so she would remember him.

The search through time had left him tired, his mind reeling. Fuck, how could she keep this up? He would have thought...

Hell, what did he think?

Chapter Two

Margo stood in front of the door, room 411. Her hand hovered at the wood but she didn't make contact. She turned, walking down the hall to the elevator.

I can't do it.

You have to.

No, I'm just not cut out to have sex with any man who wants to pay for it.

Think of your little girl.

The elevator doors opened then closed while she stood, frozen to the carpet. Snapping out of the spell she'd seemingly been under, she jammed the button with a finger.

I'm not doing this.

You have to.

The doors opened for a second time and she stepped inside. Then leaning against the mirrored wall, she watched the lights on the panel and the numbers as she descended to ground floor.

When she stepped from the lift, the lobby smelled of cleaning solution and lemon wax.

She turned and looked at the doors closing then smoothed her skirt. A long deep breath followed before her eyelids flickered. The lobby was filled with chatter and laughter.

Needing the courage to move forward, she clenched her fists and pushed the button to reopen the doors.

You will live through this and you will be able to keep your child fed. The pizza from last night is gone and there is only milk and bread in the fridge. She rubbed her arms as if she could warm herself while she moved upward. Once again she stepped into the hallway. Nothing had changed. The floor was still empty, cold, and unwelcoming.

She reached room 411 and before she could talk herself out of meeting the man behind the door, she knocked. The door opened and she gasped for breath.

"Why hello, pretty lady. I've been waiting for you."

"Carr?" Relief flooded her. Not once had she thought the man she was supposed to escort tonight would be him.

"Who did you expect?" He leaned nonchalantly against the doorframe, his easy pose erasing her fear.

"Not you." But she was so happy Carr stood in front of her, she couldn't put her feelings into words. "Are you going to invite me in or do you plan on just standing there and staring at me?" She wanted to know more about this man, why he was in Tahoe, how long he meant to stay. The list of unanswered questions grew as she thought.

His dimples appeared as if by magic, his grin so infectious she couldn't help but smile back. "Of course." He moved aside. "Come, the champagne is cold." His hand touched the small of her back.

She stepped inside, shrugging out of her wrap. He helped her and let it slide on a nearby chair.

"Thank you." She accepted the filled glass he handed her and sipped. "It's good." Relaxing seemed impossible but she tried. Walking to sliding doors leading to the balcony, she looked out on the picturesque view of the lake. Moonlight shimmered across the water. Thoughts of the night before and the coldness she'd encountered made her turn away.

Carr stood beside her. She felt the warmth of his body next to hers. He rested one hand on her shoulder and somehow that comforted her. Remembering her husband and the feelings they had shared, she knew precautions must be made. His presence had never comforted her or relaxed her and perhaps that was why she'd known when he turned traitor and given up her hiding place.

"I grew up in the Sierra Madres with my family. They have a ranch and a small mining company." He offered information, and she wondered if he wanted her to reciprocate.

"Is this my cue to tell you my life story? Trust me the tale is not interesting."

Unfortunately, it wasn't that the saga wasn't interesting. What happened to her was unbelievable, and she didn't ever mean to tell anyone.

"Nope, you'll have to cross that bridge when you get there." He laughed. "Me, I want to tell you everything about my life, who I am and where I came from."

Leaning against the window, she sipped her drink again. She wondered if the alcohol would give her courage or make her stupid. Some times it was a fine line between the two. "Everything might be more than I want to know. Over sharers can be boring or frightening."

"Probably." He shrugged, his smile wider. "I'm sure you don't want to hear all my childhood exploits. If I even border on telling you more than you want to hear, speak up and I'll stop."

At a loss for words, she sat down on the sofa. "I had a family a long time ago." Even to herself she sounded wistful. In all honesty she wanted what he had, mourned every second of the day for her lost parents. They had been deceived and paid with their lives. The news had come to her accidentally and she'd cried for hours.

"Have they passed on?" Carr sat down beside her and draped an arm across the top of the couch.

She nodded. "What seems a lifetime ago." It was longer than a lifetime. In truth, centuries had passed as she'd traveled through time to escape the demon that stalked her.

"I'm sorry. Some time if you like, I can take you to the ranch. You'd like my brothers and sisters."

"You have siblings?" She had been an only child, loved and spoiled, but she'd always felt as if she had missed out on life. Having a brother or sister to cherish and play with would have been spectacular.

"Yup." He smoothed a wisp of hair behind her ear. "I've two brothers and a set of incorrigible and fearless twin sisters. What about you?"

"None." She touched his cheek with a finger, loving the rough stubble on his jawline. Warmth seemed to flow around them. He could not be evil but he could be changed. She knew first hand how it would happen. Getting close to this man and risking everything wasn't possible. She drew back slightly, creasing her brows as she studied the man in front of her.

A knock at the door startled her. In an easy catlike motion, Carr rose from the couch, striding to the door. Her breath caught in her throat, her body tensing in fear. He didn't seem to notice her terror.

"Your order." The man pushed a table loaded with food inside. "Hope everything is fine."

Carr tipped the attendant. "Thanks."

Margo's fingers unclasped, realizing this was innocuous. The aromas emanating from the cart were heart warming. Her stomach growled and she almost laughed at herself. Carr could do that to her; help her feel safe and even lighten her dark mood. But she wasn't safe and she never would be. Her fate was written in the stars and she didn't think it would ever change.

"I ordered..."

"Oh, is that Greek salad and chicken souvlaki?" Margo lifted another lid. "Spinach and artichoke dip, my favorites. You wonderful man, it smells divine. How did you know?"

He shrugged. "Lucky guess I suppose." He plopped a piece of chicken into his mouth and chewed. "Hungry?"

She nodded. "Famished." She'd had nothing to eat since last night's pizza. Carr was a godsend to her.

Carr filled a plate for Margo and one for himself. "It's a beautiful night. Let's eat on the balcony."

Trusting him was becoming second nature to her. She needed to find someone who could help her and understand who she was, but no one would believe her. Her tale was made up of too much fantasy. So bizarre, if she told the story too many times they'd lock her up and throw away the key.

"All right." She followed Carr outside. A soft breeze blew from the lake and the moonlight shimmered on the surface, making it seem magical. "It's so beautiful. I could look at this all night long."

"Not as beautiful as you."

Heat flooded her face. She wasn't used to compliments but this one sounded sincere. "Is that your best pick-up line?"

"Oh, I've got better."

"Really." She didn't like the idea of him using pick-up lines on other women. He had a past, but did she want to be part of his future? So where was this sudden jealousy coming from?

"Truly, but after meeting you I just might stop using them."

She wasn't sure how to reply to that statement. Thinking of him with other women wasn't sitting right with her. "What kind of work do you do?"

"A safe question." He dunked a piece of chicken in the honey mustard sauce, looking to the ceiling as if he had to think about it. "My family owns a mining company in the Sierra Madres, but I run the ranch. By big bro takes care of the mine."

"Ranch—what do people do who run ranches?" She'd lived in Colorado, heard talk of dude ranches and cattle ranches, but had never seen one first hand. In her country, people kept sheep herds but not on ranches.

"Actually, I just hand out orders. We raise mostly horses but we have some cattle."

She toyed with the food on her plate, wishing she could tell him about her parents. "And I'm a glorified escort." She'd been lucky. The guy who'd bought her time the night before would have been horrific. She couldn't imagine sex with him and if Carr hadn't stepped in...

The thought dangled in her mind with no conclusion. "So, tell me why are you here? In Tahoe?"

"My birthday present from Lyn."

Margo squinted her eyes together in concentration. "Lyn?"

"One of the twins." Carr rose. Picking up both plates, he walked into the room and set them on the cart. "I saved the best for last."

She followed, a smile on her face. "What is it?"

"Chocolate cheese cake, smothered in whipped cream." He fingered a bit of the cream and touched her nose.

Before she could protest, he'd bent over and licked the cream from her face.

"Carr."

"Yes..."

"I think you are supposed to eat it from a plate and with a fork." He was interesting, and so far he surprised her at every turn.

"This way is more fun." He cut a piece of the cake with his fork and held the tempting morsel in front of her mouth. She opened for him, and he fed her the chocolate dessert.

"Ummm..."

"May I?" He was so close to her she could smell the tangy scent of his aftershave and something that was pure male animal.

"May you what?" She guessed what he asking, yet she didn't really want to admit to the fact. She didn't want to play games with him either.

"Kiss you."

With a gentleness she'd never felt before, he placed both hands on the sides of her face and with his thumbs touched her lips. Her eyes wide open, she stared into his amber green, almond shaped eyes ringed with golden lashes. His very presence filled her with self-assurance.

She nodded.

"Say the word, please." His thumbs moved across her face, touched the sides of her lips and pulled.

"Yes."

His mouth descended while they looked at each other. She didn't want to close her eyes because the expression she saw in his was tenderness and she needed to savor the picture and remember it throughout her life. He hesitated a moment before touching her mouth with his.

And when he did, she spun through time, feeling the sensation straight to the tips of her toes. Her mind went blank and she needed this feeling to last forever, through centuries. Was he the one man meant for her? She'd never believed in soul mates. In her time the women were all betrothed to any man who would gain a political advantage from the union. She'd never thought to be loved or feel this way.

What did she know about love? Nothing, so this could not mean anything. It was just a precursor to sex, and she was getting paid very well to let this man do anything he wanted with her. She might as well enjoy the moment and the new sensations, because she'd never felt this way.

"Let me inside, sweetheart."

She started to speak but was stopped when his tongue swept inside her mouth. Their tongues met and danced, played until she heard herself moan with pleasure. His growl came from deep inside and rumbled upward until she felt as if she knew the essence of the man.

Margo wanted more. Her hands rose and she ran her fingers through his hair. It was soft and silky. She felt her body clench and unclench and she knew she needed more than his tongue inside her mouth. But it was too soon. She didn't know who he really was so she forced herself to remember. Emotions about love and forever had no place in her life.

But this man had the potential to change her mind.

His fingers moved down her neck and across her shoulders. They traveled down her spine and when they moved back, she felt his fingertips on her flesh. His kiss was hot; his touch a firestorm.

Caught up in the moment, she pulled his shirt from his jeans, reveling in the feel of his skin against her hands. Melting inside, she couldn't think, could only feel.

Yes, feel the flames his kiss ignited inside and the inferno his calloused fingers detonated within.

He pulled back for a moment and she cried out inside, "No, don't stop."

But he stopped so he could sweep her into his arms and carry her to the couch where his lips met hers again. Her mouth felt swollen, the mercuric heat startling her.

~ * ~

Carr trailed kisses down her neck, stopped at an earlobe to tug with gentle teeth. The reverence he felt at this moment surmounted rational thought. This woman who came to him so unexpectedly gave promise of a lifetime.

He knew she was afraid of someone. The fucker who stalked and terrified her at the same time would find out how powerful he and his clan were. Nothing and no one was going to hurt this woman of his dreams. The world would be a better place if he could find that man and take the necessary measures.

He'd never understood the idea of a soul mate but if any one could be his, it was Margo. Time would tell. He made a mental note to call the escort agency she worked for and book her for tomorrow.

He pulled back knowing he could have all of her tonight. He could seduce her but he'd never forgive himself. She had come to him expecting to have sex, but he wanted to make love to her, not fuck her and send her home. He tapped her nose with his fingertip.

"More champagne?" Carr leaned in and whispered close to her, feeling the little shiver of desire that swept through her and the heat emanating from her. He wondered if she wanted him as much as he did her.

She sat back touching her kiss-swollen lips with a delicate fingertip, her eyes wide with something that appeared to be anticipation. Suddenly he realized he wanted to paint her before he made love to her and seduce her with words as he put brush to canvas.

"No thank you. I think I've had enough." She traced the rim of the glass then set her hand in her lap.

Despite her reply, he filled her glass. "Just in case you change your mind." Leaning against the cushions, he sipped the drink and studied her, memorizing the line of her brow, the slope of her nose, the way her eyes sparkled with what he hoped was desire.

"You didn't have to stop kissing me." She picked up her glass, her fingers gripping the stem as if it were her lifeline. Her brows furrowed together as if her words set off a panic button.

Nodding toward the glass, he said, "That's why."

"I don't understand." For a brief second she looked at her glass, liquid bubbly then back to him.

"You're terrified. Look at the death grip you have on that crystal." He felt sure she was about to deny the fear. "Don't lie. Whatever you do, don't lie or sugarcoat your feelings. I know there is a lot about your past, about you, you don't want to tell me but don't lie to me."

"You paid for me—for sex. It's your right." She closed her eyes for a moment. *You can do whatever you want.*

"The money I sent the service was for an escort and for entertainment. There is nothing in the contract that says…" He clenched his jaw but didn't speak the words that *you have to spread your legs for me.*

"No, you're right but it's implied. Now what do you want to do since you've found me lacking?" She chugged back a huge gulp of the champagne. "I don't know how to entertain, can't sing or dance. Don't know how to play the piano or any other instrument."

"Fuck, I didn't say that—mean to suggest." Anger at himself and his callous lack of regard for her feelings, had him cursing. "Good God, I would never force you to do anything."

"Don't get mad at something that is true. Admit it, if I were anyone else, we'd be beneath the sheets right now. So tell me. Why not me?" Her demand made him think.

Why not her?

"You're probably right but you are different and in a good way.

Where did you say your family lived?" He had every intention of changing the subject, and if he could learn something about her, he would be a happy man.

"I didn't. My family lived in Greece." Her grip on the glass tightened. As if she needed some liquid courage, she drank again.

"You're going to break that stem if you don't set it down. And Greece has many cities. Care to narrow it down a bit?"

"It's not there anymore, the city, and please let this go. Simply put, I can't tell you."

Her back stiffened and her words were uttered with a force he'd never heard her use.

"All right." He drummed his fingers on his leg. The silence between them seemed to stretch into eternity. "My big bro Brody and I used to ride our horses into the desert just to listen to the coyotes howl at night. Then we'd pretend to be big cats and see how loud we could scream."

"Really? Was that fun?"

"Oh yeah. We set up such a ruckus one night, didn't know there were campers near by. The men ran from their tents, guns in hand to shoot us." The memory was implanted in his head and was one among many pranks he and his brother had pulled.

"Oh my, God."

"Everything turned out all right. No one was shot and by the time we finished rolling around on the ground laughing, most everyone had dressed. When we regained our wits, we high-tailed it out of there and made straight for home. A dog with its tail between its legs couldn't have run faster."

"How old were you?" She let out a little giggle then another one, gradually turning into full-blown laughter. "And you didn't get in trouble?"

"Let me think. We were sixteen and fourteen. Dad made us muck out the stalls for a month and we lost all our privileges. Makes me laugh just thinking about it." With his story telling, he might just be on the right track.

Margo grinned then let out a giggle. "I can imagine those men and how embarrassed they must have been standing naked in the moonlight, guns in hand, and realizing they were about to shoot two teenagers." She laughed again then harder, holding her stomach.

He reached over to her to tickle her. Her scent was a bit citrus and vanilla mixed together and it knocked his socks off. "I like to see you happy, hear your laughter."

"Carr, stop." She wiggled away from him, but he wasn't about to let her go.

"Say please." He pulled her close, tickling her more. They were both laughing so hard they fell off the couch onto the floor. He landed with her on top of him then quickly rolled over. She was laughing so hard tears were in her eyes. He kissed a drop then another.

"Your tears are salty." His arms were braced on either side of her. He kissed her again then pulling back, he looked into her eyes. He kissed the tip of her nose before helping her to the couch, wishing he didn't have to let her go.

"What do you say when you give out orders? You know, are you nice or mean?" She had brought her knees to her chest.

He knew it was a protective gesture. She'd just given him something he didn't think she gifted anyone else with in a very long time, her laughter. "They all think I'm the nicest employer they've ever had."

"Really. You aren't being just a little bit arrogant? Is it hard work being a real cowboy?"

He shrugged. "Not work if you like what you do. We raise horses mostly and have a few cattle. Hmm... I told you that before. Would you like to visit sometime?" If her stalker came any closer, he wouldn't give her and her daughter a choice. He'd circle the wagons, and call out the troops before bringing her home where she'd be safe.

"Might be fun." She smiled again, a wistful looking smile.

"So tell me, you look so pensive. What are you thinking about?" He watched her move from the couch to the sliding glass doors in front of his balcony.

She leaned her head against the pane. "My family. They're gone. Dead for so many years I've lost count."

He watched from the sofa, unsure where to go with this, but he needed to know everything. "What happened to them?"

"They died a long time ago and it was my fault. I didn't think he would kill them. Phaedra said..."

He walked to her side and rested his hand on her shoulder, hoping to reassure. "What did Phaedra tell you? And who is this woman who has such a hold on your thoughts."

She turned so he could look into her eyes. This time instead of seeing tears of joy, he saw sorrow. The sparkle had vanished. "I used to laugh with Phaedra just like we did here in this room. I don't know what happened to her, but I'm sure she perished with everyone else, my parents, my friends and their servants. The people of the city where I grew up."

Servants? Her parents were wealthy then. He was sure she'd accidentally let that piece of information slip. She was starting to let down her guard and that was a good thing for him.

He made a mental note to call the agency and book her for the next week, and he decided he'd take her somewhere fun tomorrow. Maybe they could gamble a little, have a nice dinner. Or would she like a movie better?

"The sun is going to rise soon. When do you need to go home?"

"I'll call the service." She retrieved her purse and pulled out her cell.

"No, I'll take you home." He had some business to take care of and the sooner he started, the sooner he could take a little nap. He had plans for their next meeting.

"You don't need..."

"Hush, I want to be with you as long as possible." Carr pulled her into his arms for another kiss.

"Carr, I don't want to be an imposition." She seemed to hold her breath, waiting for an answer to some unspoken question.

Suddenly his hands cupped her cheeks. "Do you know how much I wanted a second kiss?"

She didn't seem to have a response. She didn't need one, because he'd no sooner said the words then he was kissing her, desperately kissing her, separating her lips, his tongue delving, tasting, and sparring with hers. He'd moved closer. Her breasts now touched his chest. And she seemed to be growing weak, leaning against him, until she finally kissed him back.

He groaned at the first sign of yielding then pulled back to look at her. Her gaze met his and went no further. Her eyes were a soft brown and seemed to question, and there was something else he couldn't define. Her lips parted, trembled, but she didn't look away.

His head bent, and he caressed her lips with his. He wanted the taste of her on his lips and in his head. He kissed her again, his tongue once more parting her lips to delve inside. He was on the very edge of losing the ability to think. Her eagerness inflamed him, made him fight for the control he was so used to having with other women.

He'd promised himself he would get to know her before he made love with her. The sex was not as important as the feeling, he reminded himself. Fuck, he didn't want to let her go or take her home.

She has a daughter who needs her. I need her.

The sun peeked its head over the trees and mountains. Light shimmered through the balcony doors. "I need to get you home."

Margo leaned her head against his chest while he rubbed her back. If she felt the same way he did...

Well he'd let that question hang in the air.

"I know." She looked up. "I want to be home when Sophie wakes up."

"Sophie, that's your little girl?"

"Yes..."

"Well then, gather your belongings and I'll drive you home. And we don't need to have that argument again. You're not calling the service." He'd have his way in this.

Twenty minutes later, he pulled up in front of her home and turned off the car. "I'll see you tonight."

Her eyes widened but she didn't say anything for a few seconds. Moments later, she stepped from the car. Then the door burst open and Sophie raced down the sidewalk, arms flung wide to greet her mother.

Margo threw her arms open, lifting Sophie in a giant bear hug then whirling her around in the air.

"Mama, I woke up early and was so sad to find out you weren't at home. Are you going to stay home tonight? You promised me."

"I was at work." She set Sophie on the ground. "And I can't promise, you know that. I told you if I didn't get work, I'd stay home."

A huge lump formed in Carr's throat. Embarrassment swept through him, an emotion he hadn't felt in a very long time. He meant to do something about Margo's plight and soon. He then reformed his plans for the evening to come.

"Do you work with that man?" Sophie pointed at him.

He felt like ducking down behind the steering wheel. Instead, he waved and smiled at the little girl.

"Yes. Yes I do. Come on, have you eaten breakfast yet?" Margo wrapped an arm around her girl and walked to the house. When she opened the door, Margo turned and waved at him. He nodded then turned the ignition.

He had a list a mile long to accomplish before he saw her next.

~ * ~

At a point overlooking the lake, Carr parked his car before pulling out his cell phone. It took some time but he was able to find out the name of the person Margo rented from and jot down the phone as well as the number for her nanny. It was still too early to call her landlord or the nanny, so he dialed the number to the escort agency and made an appointment for ten o'clock.

The sun shone brilliantly on the lake and the warm weather beckoned to him. A run would be nice and might clear his head. He had so many thoughts swimming in his mind and so many things he needed to accomplish, it was hard for him to settle down.

He turned the ignition on and backed out of the parking lot. He headed to his favorite wooded place in Tahoe, one where people seldom frequented. Fifteen minutes later, he'd turned onto an isolated dirt road. Filled with potholes and rocks, the ride was bumpy but at this moment Carr didn't care. Quickly exiting the vehicle, he walked into the forest until he could no longer see the road. He undressed, felt energy synthesize within his core. His body shook as he shifted from the tips of his toes to the top of his head. Suddenly he stood on all fours and took in a deep breath.

He padded back to the road then found the animal trail that headed toward the lake. At first he walked slowly, feeling his muscles warm and his body relax into his new form.

Shit this feels good.

Picking up speed, he ran, brush and high grass whipped around him. Exhilaration filled his soul. Wind whistled around his head, tickling his ears. This pace he could hold for only a short time. A sprinter not a long distance runner, he slowed and lumbered to a rock above the lake.

The sun beat down and warmed the boulder. He curled up and let his chin rest on his paws. A short catnap in the warm fall sun was in order. Ah, the heat absorbed by his golden-black fur, made him purr. He twitched his tail with the feelings of pleasure.

Thirty minutes later, he was dressed and in his car. The agency for his ten am appointment was his destination. Ten minutes later, he pulled into the parking lot and exited his car. Long strides brought him to the office.

"Carr McKenna here." He leaned on the desk, both hands resting on the polished granite surface. He slanted the receptionist a lopsided grin then to her nameplate. "Sara?"

She smiled back at him, batting her lashes. "Down the hall, second door on the left, just knock."

"Thanks." He followed her directions, scrutinizing the doors lining the hallways and memorizing the names and the numbers.

His hand rose to knock.

"Come in." The lady on the other side of the door called out to him. He looked to the ceiling above and noticed the security cameras.

Once inside, he studied the woman on the other side of the desk who rose, holding out her hand.

He politely obliged.

"How can I be of help?" She fingered through a file folder on her desk.

"You know, Margo..." he began then wished he knew her last name.

"Margo Cunningham?"

"I think so. Do you have a photo?" Damn, that sounded lame. He should have pursued it last night at dinner. But she avoided questions like the plague and he had a strong belief that Cunningham wasn't her real last name.

"How do I know you're legit?" Her hand rested protectively on the folder, voice firm.

At that moment he wasn't sure he was going get what he wanted. "You don't. But I want Margo for the next two and a half weeks and I'm damn sure not going to put down a wad on someone who isn't my Margo." He felt better already.

Her brows knitted together. "I really shouldn't."

"But you will, for the money." Getting what he wanted wasn't always what he wanted. He thought there would be more security here. That the madam would question him a bit more, ask for ID or something. But it seemed she was going to hand over her file to him.

"Of course, this is, after all, about the money." She held up the picture.

Air rushed from his lungs. Relief at the sight in front of him was tangible. "It's her."

"Good, when I see the money, I'll fill her calendar with your name."

He pulled out his wallet and flipped the money on her desk. "Count it."

A minute later she looked up, a grin on her face. "It's all here." She pulled a spreadsheet on her computer and found Margo Cunningham then typed Carr's name in every slot for the next two and one half weeks.

"Now you can erase her name from this ledger." Carr was confident he would win her over and he didn't want anyone else getting near Margo.

The madam turned to Carr one eyebrow raised. "The lady doesn't have a say in this?"

Of course she did. "By the time this is done, she'll agree that I'm the best thing who ever came into her life."

"Hmm... confident aren't you, big guy? But it doesn't work that way. This is a business and I'm making money with your lady. It's going to cost."

"How much?"

She jumped. "Don't growl at me."

"How much?"

"Ten thousand would do." She turned back to the computer.

"How long is she contracted for?"

"Now that's not your business."

"I can ask her."

"Of course, but she's not in this room right now and I think this deal needs to be settled before you leave."

"I'll give you two thousand and not a penny more." He had a hunch Margo hadn't contracted as long as he'd just bought her time."

"That'll do," she said.

He flipped the bills on her desk. "Give me her folder and I want a receipt."

"Anything for you, big guy," she purred.

When she said that he knew she'd bilked him for more money than she'd signed for but he didn't care. Margo was his.

Next stops, the rental agency and the nanny service. He finished at those places with fewer complications, managing to pay Margo's rent and her nanny for the next three weeks.

He wanted to see her face when she found out what he'd done. He grinned, pleased with himself.

Chapter Three

Two days later and in a rage, Margo swept through the lobby of the hotel. A funnel cloud of heat swirled around her. The inferno penetrating her body simmered soul deep.

Calm yourself.

Breathe.

Calm yourself.

She stopped at a drinking fountain to drink the cooling water. *Breathe... Think of the summer blue sky and cool mountain breezes.*

Believing she had her emotions under control, she quickly made her way to the elevator. The shiny silver gray metal caught images behind her as the people went about their business.

He paid my rent—bought my contract at the agency—paid off my nanny. How dare he! An inferno of wrath swept through her. Inside she felt as if she boiled.

Suddenly a garbage can outside the hotel burst into flames. The elevator metal caught the reflection. She turned, her breath catching in her throat. The attendant at the desk grabbed a fire extinguisher and rushed outside. In minutes the fire had died to embers, but the one inside Margo simmered, waiting for release.

She punched the elevator button then pushed it again and again.

Damn him. Damn, damn and double damn. I'm not going to let Carr McKenna fuck with my life.

Doors in front of her opened. She stepped inside and punched the number four circle. Stepping back, she clasped and unclasped her hands, closed her eyes, inhaled long and deep. Nothing seemed to cool her body or quiet her rollercoaster emotions.

A few minutes later, she raised her hand to knock on Carr's door. Before she saw him, she needed to tamp down the rising anger. She needed to think of something else. Sophie, so pretty when she left her playing with the nanny. She'd dumped the crayons out of the box and was drawing pictures of their house.

Stay cool, stay calm, you have to do this.

By the time Carr opened the door, she was shaking from head to toe. On wobbly legs, she stepped inside.

"You look beautiful."

She whirled around, her hands clenching into tight fists. His smile and his dimples infuriated her more, her breathing quick and shallow. Unable to regulate what she was feeling and before she could stop herself, she swung as hard as she could, slapping Carr on the cheek.

"I hate you." But she didn't hate him. She abhorred what he'd done.

Silence lingered for a few seconds. His smile vanished as he put his hand on his cheek. One eyebrow rose a fraction.

"A... What did I do?" He rubbed his face, his eyes wide with seeming curiosity. His dimples had vanished for a moment but now they were back.

"I will not be your mistress or your whore." She jabbed a finger at his chest, hoping the violence against him would make her feel better.

His arms went out in a gesture that seemed to say confusion. "I have no idea what you're talking about."

"I won't be kept." She didn't think the heat inside would evaporate. The inferno grew out of proportion.

"You need to explain to me..."

She stepped up to him, her hands on his chest. "You bought my contract and ended it. You paid my rent and the nanny. I will not be bought."

"I was just trying to help." Once again, he spread his arms wide, a gesture that seemed to question.

"That's not..."

The receipts in the ashtray flamed. "Oh my, God." She raced to the bathroom and splashed cold water on her face, cupped it in her hands and drank. Nothing was working. More water on her face then she grabbed a glass. After filling it, she dumped the glass on top of her head. Water dripped down her face and onto her clothes. One more dousing and she might feel sane again, the flames within quenched.

When she turned, Carr stood in the doorway, hands on its frame. He stared at her as if she were crazy.

"I'm sorry..." She stepped by him when he turned to give her room to pass. The fire was out. Arms crossed, she sat down on the couch. Not wanting to look at him, she stared at the charred remains in the ashtray.

"You all right?" He stood in front of her.

Her gaze remained focused away from Carr. "No, I'm not all right or fine or anything else." For a moment she thought she could pretend ignorance of the fire, but somehow she knew Carr wouldn't believe her.

He sat down beside her and took her hand in his. The protectiveness of the gesture amazed her.

"You're a firestarter."

That caught her attention and she looked up. His statement wasn't a question. "You know about firestarters?"

He nodded. "I know a lot about the paranormal and I've researched magical creatures. But what I don't understand is why you seem to have no control. That fire below my balcony, you started that one too?"

"I didn't mean... I was so angry with you. The rage overcame me and I can't control it because I was never taught. When I left, I was given paper directions but that's not the same as instruction."

Carr's thumb rubbed gentle circles on the top of her hand. His simple gesture soothed her tattered emotions and made her relax. Tears formed in her eyes. "When did you leave and from where?"

She brushed the moisture from her cheeks. "It doesn't matter."

"Come here." He pulled her into his arms. Her head rested against his chest. "You have cooled down a bit."

The slow beating of his heart eased the rage she'd felt. She nodded. "I can't stay mad at you for very long."

His hands swept through her wet hair then down her back. "That's good." He laughed, and she felt a gentle awakening.

"I'm going to pay you back all that money." She had to do the right thing but she also had to admit his interference put food on the table for the next two weeks.

"If that's what you want."

"It is." She pushed off his chest. Her gaze focused on him, she tried to reach inside his mind.

"I'm not sorry for helping you. I know you don't understand my reasons, but I didn't mean to make you believe I was buying your favors. Well I am, but not the way you think."

"How do I think?" The challenge shook her. She didn't know where that came from. His sigh and ensuing frown made her regret what she'd asked.

He wanted to change the subject. "Were your parents firestarters?"

In his arms, she stiffened and she felt him tighten his hold, protecting, taking care of her. "I think so. They never spoke of it. But Phaedra, the servant they sent with me, had papers for me to read when I was old enough. The documents had to come from somewhere."

He hugged her tight. The tattoo on his arms flexed, as she traced the figure of the golden-black jaguar.

"How old were you when your parents sent you away?" He kissed her forehead.

She closed her eyes and snuggled into him. "I was six."

"The same as your daughter."

"Yes." Pain at her loss swept through her. The thought of losing her daughter now would devastate her. She wondered how her parents had dealt with losing her. And how had they felt when they learned she'd fled?

"That must have been hard."

The warmth of his body next to hers kept her sane and gave her hope. "I never understood why. Phaedra tried to tell me, but nothing made sense until I finally had to escape."

"Margo, I believe there is so much more to this story. I'm not going to push you but if you are still in danger, the more I know the easier it will be for me to protect you."

Her laugh sounded brittle to her ears. "Unless you have supernatural powers, there is nothing you can do. All I ask is that you try your best not to betray me."

"Never." He pulled her close, kissing her quickly on the forehead. "And we'll talk more about the unbelievable, but first I want to ask you a question. Is it all right with you if I give you a gift? It's just something little I picked up this afternoon. Thought it might be easier for us to stay in contact."

She squinted her eyes. "Are you afraid I'm going to set something on fire again?"

"Maybe. I do value my life." He moved from the couch to his desk where he opened a drawer and pulled out a small object.

Her curiosity peaked. "What is it?"

He held it up. "A new iPhone, see." He strode back to the couch and sat down next to her.

"I..." She swallowed hard. "I've never been given anything this nice. I don't think I should accept. It's too much."

"No." He tried to give it to her.

She pushed it away. "I don't want to be obligated to you in anyway." Moisture welled in her eyes. She didn't want to cry. She wasn't going to cry. Why would a simple gift make her so emotional?

"No strings attached." He set the cell phone in front of her. "I don't want anything in return."

"If it sounds too good to be true, it usually is." She picked up the phone, turning it over in her hands. "I don't even know how to use it."

Carr took it from her and showed her how to turn it on. "It has a security code. I typed in the numbers of the room where we first me plus a zero. You can change it if you want."

"2-0-0-7" She swiped the window then pushed the numbers and the face lit up with little boxes. "What are these?"

Smiling, he gave her a lesson in cell phone use 101. "I put in my contact number for you and I have your phone number in my cell." He held it up. "See."

She nodded, perplexed and trying to remember everything he'd told her. He'd showed her how to text. Not too hard since he was the only one in her list. It was sad she had no friends, but she decided she'd ask her nanny for her number then she could check up on Sophie whenever she wanted.

She tried it out and texted him. His phone beeped. She looked up, smiling. "Was that me?"

"It was. By George, you got the hang of it. You're a natural." He picked her up off her feet and whirled her around the room for several minutes. They fell on the couch together, Carr on top of her, his arms bracing her so his weight didn't smother her.

When she gazed at him, beautiful amber-green eyes looked back. She moistened her lips, hoping for a kiss and maybe more, never understanding why he paid so much for her services, and didn't take what was his right.

His lips met hers. She heard him groan, felt muscles deep inside her clench. His tongue moistened her lips then traced the seam. Leaving her mouth, he kissed her cheek, her ear, tugging on the lobe then her nose and down her neck. He teased her, and she purred with delight.

She felt cherished; another new-to-her feeling. Kissing his way across her collarbone, and slipping the tiny strap to her dress down so he could find bare shoulder, she ran her fingers through his hair.

"Carr..."

"Yes," he whispered.

He found her lips again and delved inside. Their tongues touched and dueled. She was in heaven.

The kiss was over before she could open her eyes. "Don't stop."

"Are you hungry? I am and I promised you dinner and a night on the town."

"When did you do that?" He pulled her to a sitting position. "Not since I walked into the room ready to set the world on fire—literally."

"How about right now. Want to go out to dinner then try your hand at gambling?"

"I don't have the money to gamble." Yet she thought it might be fun. At the moment she'd just be throwing her money away and she wasn't foolish. She'd learned that over the years.

"I can give you some." He strode to his jacket that had been draped over the couch and slipped it on then tossed her the wrap she'd worn.

"There you go again, trying to take care of me. How about if I watch you throw away your money." She liked the sexy grin he slanted her.

"I'm good at cards and I don't usually lose. I know when to quit."

"You don't lose? I thought all the games were in the house's favor."

He shrugged, looped an arm around her waist. "But if you're good at math and count cards then you have a good chance to win sometimes."

"You can do this, count cards and why am I surprised you're good at math."

He laughed. "Why indeed?"

Carr stepped aside to let her pass through the door. A few minutes later they were on the street. She stared at the poor garbage can that had caught the wrong end of her wrath.

"What do you feel like eating? Food first, gambling second or would you rather go for a carriage ride?" Carr nodded his head toward a horse-drawn carriage.

"I'd rather stay inside." The thought of the ice demon finding her sent a chill spiraling within. "I'm safer inside."

"Ok then, we'll eat, at least walk through the hotels where they gamble, maybe pull a one-armed bandit then head back to my room. I have something I want to show you."

~ * ~

"Order anything you like." Carr gazed at the menu for a moment. He knew what he wanted. When he looked up, he studied the room. He sat with his back to the wall so he could observe the people coming and going in the restaurant.

He felt as if all eyes in the room watched Margo, and he didn't like the feeling. The emotion wasn't jealousy but something that welled up from deep inside and tried to take over his entire soul.

"Carr...Carr." Margo placed her hand on his. "Carr, whatever are you thinking?"

Heat rushed to his face. He was suddenly and unexplainably self-conscious, but there was no reason for embarrassment. "I was," he turned her hand over in his and traced one of the lines on her palm, "thinking about you, only you sweet darlin'."

"Then a penny for your thoughts."

He cleared his throat. "You are the most beautiful woman, inside and out. I want to spend a lot more time with you, and keep you safe from whoever stalks you."

The waiter was at their table, pen and paper in hand. "Can I get you something to drink?"

"What would you like?" Carr squeezed Margo's hand.

"A glass of white wine, a riesling."

The waiter nodded.

"Same for me."

"Are you ready to order?"

Carr waited for Margo. "How about the chicken in orange sauce, with rice and a salad."

"Good choice."

"Then I'll have the same." Carr folded the menu and handed it to the waiter. Turning his attention to Margo, he said, "You seem relaxed, are you?"

"More than when I walked in your door." Her laughter had him grinning like an idiot.

"Well that isn't saying much. On a scale of one to ten, how do you feel? Ten being the most tranquil."

"Let me think about this. Maybe a seven." She smiled. "But after my glass of wine the number might change to an eight."

The bartender set their glasses on the table.

"Here's to finding the man you're running from and making sure he's punished." Carr held his glass in the air for the toast. What he didn't tell her was he meant to end the man. She probably wanted the same thing but was unwilling to voice it.

"Amen," she said, her eyes wide open. "I don't doubt your intentions are good but he is a fierce adversary. You could get hurt, and I couldn't forgive myself."

"I'm sure I've dealt with worse." He remembered the Amazonian devil he, his brother and his sister had defeated a little over a year ago. God, but his sister had nearly died that day. But in the end they'd won and that devil was dead. Sadie, the woman they were protecting, had lived and married Brody. Margo was someone he could tell this story.

"Really? You don't know anything about this guy. I don't want to talk about it tonight. If it's possible, I want to forget for the time I'm with you."

"When then? I need to know..."

She put a finger to his lips to stop the next words. "Please."

"All right." It seemed she was saved by the arrival of the salads as well as his willingness to oblige her wishes. He would do whatever she asked. He laughed and knew just how tight she'd wrapped him around her needs. The feeling was one he didn't ever want to lose.

"Pepper?" The waiter held the pepper grinder.

"Yes," they both said.

God she was so delicate. She even ate with tiny little bites. He was a giant of a man, and they were such opposites.

They ate in silence. She didn't talk, and all he wanted to know was what he'd just promised not to pursue.

It wasn't long before Carr paid the check and they were leaving the restaurant. "I'll spot you ten dollars and you play the one-armed bandit until you win or lose it all."

"I want to argue, but you're not going to take no for an answer are you?" She shot him a grin that melted his heart.

Carr shook his head. "Nope." One hand rested on the small of her back while he ushered her outside. "You're shaking."

She smushed her lips together. "I've never done anything like this. I guess I'm excited and overwhelmed as well as worried about paying you back."

"I'm going to give you new experiences whenever I can. And my sweet darlin', it's only ten dollars." He hoped she'd forget about paying him back, but something strange down the street drew his focus away from Margo.

An older man, with graying hair and wearing a trench coat, was making a point of stopping people. He would ask a question then move on. Carr would give just about anything to know what the man asked, but he wasn't going to take a chance with Margo. This could be her stalker or someone who wasn't dangerous, but he did not want to chance an encounter.

Taking her hand, he said, "Let's go that way." They turned, and she slanted him a curious looking glare.

"Why?"

"Because I don't like that man down the street. I have this sixth sense he doesn't mean you well."

"Fuck." The word was little more than a whisper but Carr heard it.

He was shocked, not by the word, but that she'd said it. He wanted to throw his head back and let out a bellow of laughter, but he didn't want to draw attention to himself.

Heat from Margo encompassed his hand. Good, she was more angry than afraid. She needed the rage and she needed to practice. "Control it."

She nodded. "Right."

He pulled her close and wrapped an arm around her shoulder. Touching more of her body, he'd know how well she did. "Breathe deep, think of the cool lake swirling around you."

She nodded. "I'm remembering the dousing of water I gave myself a few hours ago in your room."

He couldn't get that picture from his head. Her blouse plastered against her body, he could see her curves outlined exquisitely. "That's better. It's working."

They strolled into a casino. Walking around the room, he pointed out various games until they ended up at the dollar machine.

He handed her ten one dollar bills and pulled out the same for himself. Showing her how to use what he hoped was a winning combination of plays, he let her try it all out.

"Here goes." After betting all of her money, she punched in some pictures then pulled the lever. The colors spun by. She picked up her purse, ready to leave, but the machine whirled then made noise, and when Carr pointed to the slot machine, she saw all of the pictures lined up in a row.

She'd almost doubled her money.

"Keep playing." Carr enjoyed watching her, the animation on her face, the way she crinkled her brow when she focused.

"Really? But..." She pulled the arm again and watched the pictures whirl. It didn't seem as if she could lose.

"Good job." Carr wasn't playing. Looking at her was more fun.

Margo pulled her lip beneath her top teeth, squinting at the machine. Carr almost lost it and laughed but he kept that feeling in check. He leaned against the back of the seat, crossing his arms in front of him.

Time seemed to stand still. At least an hour later, she looked up at him, her expression a bit sheepish. "I'm done."

"You won a lot of money." He pulled the ticket from the machine. "Let's go cash it in."

"I really did win. I don't even like to gamble, still don't. Why don't you keep the money?"

He did laugh then. "You're crazy. I didn't win and I don't need money. You do. And if you don't like my helping you out financially, friend to friend, then you need this."

They stood in front of the desk, waiting for the cash. After the man cashed them out, she handed Carr a ten-dollar bill.

He stuck his hands in his pockets and shook his head.

She waved it at him then pushed it inside his back pocket. "You're not going to take no for an answer?"

"Nope." Let's go back to my place. I've something to show you."

Darkness had fallen several hours ago and now the moon cast it's light on the city as well as the lake. A slight breeze brought the perfume of flowers. For a moment, Carr closed his eyes, all his thoughts were directed at protecting Margo. He wanted to encapsulate her in an armor barrier that would keep her safe from everything.

He laughed to himself, thinking about her abilities. That armor would have to be made of fireproof steel or she'd melt it when her anger overcame control.

He caught a chill on the wind and tried to take it into himself. He must have succeeded because she didn't shiver or notice the dip in temperature. Making a mental note to ask his great grandfather about this, he searched the street for any sign of danger. And remembering the man with the graying hair, he looked for him.

He saw nothing.

She inhaled a long deep breath, a smile on her face. "What was it you said you were going to show me?"

"Curious?" He hugged her close, enjoying everything about her.

"Yes, I am. It can't be as crazy as my starting fires."

"Don't bet on it. I think it's on the same level." He wasn't too sure how to proceed. Stripping in front of her had its merits but it would scare her. He could explain what he was going to do. Maybe he could disappear in the bedroom and come out a jaguar. The mire he was in grew deeper with each thought.

The only way he was sure he could convince her that he'd actually changed was to shift in front of her.

Her laughter was good to hear. He'd been able to coax the smiles and amusement from her. The longer she went without feeling the cold, the more happiness she'd have. Once more, thoughts of protection flowed from him and he prayed into her.

Into the hotel and up the elevator to his room, it seemed to happen way too fast. In a few moments his deepest secret, one that few people knew about would be revealed to Margo. If she were human, he'd be afraid of so much more, disgust, fear, and disbelief.

But with Margo he didn't know what to expect.

"We're here." She sounded enthusiastic.

Perhaps at his expense, but he pointed her to the couch. "Sit."

He knelt down beside her, taking her hand.

"You're scaring me."

"I don't mean to." Frightening her was the last intention. "I want you to listen to what I have to say. I won't hurt you. I promise."

Her eyes were wide but he wasn't sure if it was fear or curiosity.

"What are you going to do?" She squeezed his hand. "I shouldn't but I trust you. And I pray every day you won't turn on me. So I'm going to have faith in you now."

"Have you heard of people who can manifest themselves into different forms?"

She looked down at her hands then back up. "No."

"They are called shapeshifters. And that is what I am and it's why I was surprised to see you start a fire but not too alarmed. I know there are people, demons, magical creatures in the world. Mostly we hide, unable to talk about the powers we possess."

She smiled, and he watched her swallow before she met his gaze. "What is your other form?"

"I change into a golden-black jaguar." He held his breath while he waited for her reaction or comment.

She traced the tattoo on his arm. "This has significance then."

"You think?"

"Yeah."

"If I shift with clothes on they shred. So..."

"So you have to take them off." She finished his sentence for him.

"I don't want to disrobe in front of you and I don't want to disappear into the bedroom and come back as a big cat."

"I get your dilemma. I'll close my eyes and open them when you tell me to."

"Is that different than going into the bedroom?"

"Timing?"

"I hear you." Carr unbuttoned his shirt and took off his shoes and socks. He shrugged out of the shirt, and heard her swift inhale of air. "I feel as if I'm doing a striptease. I think, my sweet darling, you can close your eyes now." His fingers went for the fastening on his jeans.

"Ok." She shut her eyes.

"Don't peek." He slipped from his jeans and felt the adrenalin surge as he started to change form. His body shook and raw energy ripped through him. Suddenly he stood on all fours and padded to Margo.

~ * ~

Phaedra stood at the window of Jokul's ice castle on top a mountain in Greenland. The building blended into the surrounding terrain, unnoticeable.

She put her hand on the slave collar around her neck. At first she didn't understand why Jokul had spared her life. So few people knew her abilities as a seer.

The first time he'd asked her to find Atantsi, she'd refused. But the ensuing torture was enough to cause her loyalty to waver. His rage had been so great he'd covered her in ice and only the house physician had been able to save her. After that, he controlled the freeze. He learned how to blanket her in frost until she turned blue.

"Phaedra, where is Atantsi? You know what I can do to you." His gravelly voice sent an unforeseen chill down her spine.

She bowed, knowing she needed to show her submissiveness. "I can't find her. There is no warmth. It is as if a protective cloak of steel has surrounded her. This has never happened before." She braced herself for the cold that was sure to come. But she felt nothing.

"Keep trying."

"Jokul..."

"I believe you. I have had the same trouble. She might have learned to cloak herself."

"Or she might have a protector." Phaedra prayed that was the case. She didn't want to find Atantsi. She needed to live in peace and wanted the same for her girlhood friend.

"Impossible. After what happened to the firefighter, she won't trust anyone."

"Of course, you are right." At her suggestion, the collar around her neck tightened. Her hand rested on it but she knew she would have to do something nice for the ice demon or he would continue to tighten the silver necklace that proclaimed her his slave.

She walked toward him, loosening the tie on her dress and let it fall to the marble beneath her feet. Her heart raced in a frenzied panic.

He settled himself on a bench and motioned her forward. "Down on your knees, my slave."

She obeyed and the collar loosened a fraction. "Yes, my highness." She hated him. Despised what he made her do. She should have killed herself a long time ago but she clung to life.

"You know what I like."

Phaedra cried frozen tears of pain and hatred, vowing revenge.

Chapter Four

Two days later when Margo stood at Carr's door, room 411 in the hotel, her new cell phone chimed. Surprised she looked at the screen and on it she read.

Door is unlocked come in.

Hands shaking, unsure of what he was up to, she pushed on the door and stepped inside. At first she didn't see anyone. She moved further inside, questioning.

Carr, in his jaguar form rubbed against her legs. The purr she heard was loud and clearly told her he enjoyed the moment. He gently nudged her toward the sofa. Grinning, she complied with what she thought were his wishes. His gestures were far from subtle.

When she sat down, he jumped up next to her, settling his large paws across her lap and leaning into her. Her heart racing and very hesitant, she placed her hand on his head and stroked his ears. "Nice kitty." *Well that was stupid.* Carr was no kitty. His tail twitched and his eyes bored into hers as if he tried to read her mind.

He put his chin on her breasts nuzzling in and purring contentedly, tail moving back and forth in a crazy rhythm. She swallowed hard, unsure of herself and his motives.

"Really?" She questioned her sanity. "You are misbehavin'. Carr, you're making me..."

He purred. And she was sure he grinned at her. When he nuzzled her shoulder, she nearly jumped out of her skin.

His teeth were at the strap of her tank top, pulling, sliding it from her shoulder where he rubbed his nose and mouth. She pushed at his face but ended up rubbing his ears and encouraging him.

"Carr, what on earth are you doing?"

With beautiful cat eyes, he stopped and looked at her. She could swear he was telling her to trust him. Then he turned his attention to the other shoulder, pulling that strap down too.

She squirmed but his massive body held her down. It wasn't that she was afraid or she didn't like what he did, but he was a cat. And if it were a little cat and if it wasn't Carr, she'd just think he was cute and cuddly. She'd pull him close and held him tight. Well the strap part didn't make sense but this was Carr, cat or human, and she felt sure Carr's sole purpose in life was to seduce her.

She pushed at him. "Carr get off." She tried for command in her voice and it sounded more like a squeak. "Carr, you've got to stop this right now, please." She truly didn't want to plead with him but she needed to see the real Carr, the human Carr.

With a swish of his tail and cat-like grace, the golden-black cat jumped from her lap and padded into the bedroom. A few minutes later, Carr, in jeans and a t-shirt, strode from the room.

She cocked her head sideways, mesmerized by the strength and power of the man—in any form.

He waggled his eyebrows at her then made himself comfortable on the couch beside her. "Sorry about that. I didn't mean to make you uncomfortable, but I couldn't resist getting my ears rubbed."

"And you think I'd only pet your ears if you were in cat form?" *Good God, where did that comment come from?* She was going insane.

He leaned in as if he wanted her to pet his ears and smirked at her. He challenged her and she didn't want to lose. Raising her hand, she played with his hair before touching his ear and running her finger around the lobe.

His hand slid up her arm to the back of her neck then pulled her close. The kiss was hard, deep and over almost before it began, yet it left her breathless. She wanted more.

"We have to talk. I have things I need to tell you, things about my family. I want you to know more about me. Before we make love."

"You mean have sex, and you're actually going to ask for what you've been paying me for this last week? I'm speechless."

"You might be when I finish. But first, are you hungry? I ordered sandwiches and I've beer in the fridge or wine if you'd prefer."

"Hungry and beer." She knew he had a history and one that could be more convoluted and weirder than hers. A part of her wanted to learn more and another part feared the newfound knowledge would bring her closer to him.

Being friends to any man terrified her. This time her apprehension wasn't for her, it was for Carr. Jokul was dangerous and from what little she knew of Carr, she was pretty sure he would protect her with his life. She didn't want anyone to die because of her.

At the table, Carr unwrapped the sandwiches. "They're both turkey on rye. Hope you like that." He uncapped a beer and handed it to her.

Confidence oozed from every pore on his sleek body. She wished she could be that self-assured. Running and hiding for so long, she feared every shadow and jumped at every noise.

Picking at her food and sipping at the cold beer, she waited for him to talk. When the silence grew too long for her liking, she asked, "What did you want to tell me?"

"Eat first," he bit into his food and watched her, his eyes taking on a deeper amber hue.

She was sure he was thinking, counting back in time, remembering his clan's history. That's what she would do.

Her mother and father were the kindest and gentlest of people. She didn't know if either or both were firestarters. They'd sent her away at such a young age, she'd never been aware of their state or abilities, magical or otherwise.

Six years old she'd been thrust into the coldest most barren land she could have ever imagined. She wrapped her arms around herself, thinking of the frozen temperatures and the frigid landscape.

She supposed some might have thought it beautiful, but she'd been so lonely and lost the first two years. Then Phaedra appeared as if from a fairy tale. The young girl had been older, but Margo didn't know how much. Phaedra had seemed so wise and shrewd, perhaps beyond her years. Later, she'd discovered her parents had sent Phaedra to take care of her.

"Lost in thought?" Carr's question startled her back to reality. He set his sandwich on the table, picking up her hand, before turning it over and tracing the lines on her palm.

She shuddered, unsure if the sensation came from the sensual pleasure Carr evoked or her thoughts. "I suppose, but if you're asking what, I'm not ready to tell. It's all too painful and too real. I promise I will tell you soon though."

"Today's my turn for truths." Letting go of her hand, he folded his napkin and set the cloth on the table. Then he took both of her hands in his, looking deep into her eyes.

"You're scaring me." She squirmed backward, tugging on her hands.

He let go. "It's just history and will give you some idea where I came from and how I think and how I view the world around me."

"That would be impossible. You continue to surprise me and as to guessing what you're thinking, well I couldn't possibly."

She watched him inhale a deep breath. It seemed he was ready to start, and she was more than ready to listen.

"It was the time before-time." He began. "The McKenna Clan lived in the highlands of Scotland. There were few people and their land stretched for many miles."

She thought a moment while he was talking, surprised to hear knowledge of the time before-time. She would tell him where she came from and soon.

"They ruled the land. The McKenna was powerful and he took care of the few people who were not of the clan. Even then they were shapeshifters. Roaming the countryside in the form of the big cat was exhilarating. But they always knew they had to keep this a secret."

"Secrets are often hard to preserve." She knew first hand how easily it was to give yourself away.

Trusting someone rarely came without a price.

"As time passed, the number of people roaming the hills, shifter and human, grew. Chance encounters became more common and the clan worried they would be discovered." With this said, Carr rose and walked to the window. His hands behind his back, he stood motionless as if frozen.

He startled her when he suddenly turned, his face a mask, void of expression.

"Were they discovered?" She prayed they were not, but it seemed they could not conceal themselves forever.

"In ways. Some were humorous when the story was told. Mostly, the shifter about to be discovered would shift back. Of course he would be butt naked and embarrassed but there was nothing that could be done. Discovery would have been worse."

"Couldn't they just stay in their cat form?" What Carr said didn't make sense to her.

"They could but they could be killed or trapped. If it got out there were black jaguars in the Highlands, the people would flock there to catch a possible glimpse of the animals."

"Then matters would be worse." She finished the sentence for him.

Silence followed. It seemed, once again, Carr was remembering, thinking perhaps about times past.

"My great grandfather, gramps we call him, remembers all of the tales of our clan as well as the Apache. He still lives on a ranch, deep in the Sierra Madre Mountains. He likes the modern conveniences but his seclusion as well."

Overwhelmed by Carr's story and the reverence in his voice when he spoke, she didn't know what to say.

"If I have no past, does that mean I have no future either?" Nausea boiled in her stomach. She swallowed in an effort to rid herself of the sickness.

"I don't think so," he spoke softly. "I believe you and I have a future together and you will eventually allow me to protect you and love you."

"Carr, I don't want..." Loving this man would be so easy but she couldn't make him vulnerable to Jokul and the dangers surrounding her.

At the signs of her first protest, he stopped her. "Hush, we will speak more of this later. But for now I'd like to finish my story. I know you have no trust in your heart, but I'm confident I can change that feeling. Right now I have more to tell you about my family, how they came to North America."

He sat on the sofa now, and Margo cuddled into him, loving the strength and the warmth he passed to her. She closed her eyes and rested her head against his chest while he circled his arm around her. "I'm listening."

"We were known throughout the Highlands as the clan Chattan which means clan of the cats, and the people grew, prospered and enjoyed their lives. Yet many grew restless. Exploration around the world had made them curious. Were there others of their kind in different parts of the globe?"

"I find this all fascinating, Carr. It's such a relief to know I'm not alone." Her fingers toyed with the buttons on his shirt. Her people had no history because of Jokul. She envied Carr and his family, wishing she could be part of something so solid.

"As long as I'm alive you will not be alone." His voice sounded so sincere, so strong.

She didn't understand the emotions coming from him. He'd turned her life upside down. "I don't see how you can make that statement and so adamantly. I'm nothing to you and I never will be."

"In time, just give it time and I'll convince you." He pulled her close for a quick hug.

"Many years passed and it was no longer the time before time. It was the nineteenth century. The clan had developed and flourished. Yet many had the wanderlust in their souls. They saw clipper ships disappearing on the horizon and many wondered what was on the other side of the sunset. Like countless young people of all times, they wanted to spread their wings and become independent."

"So," she pushed off from his chest to look into his eyes, beautiful amber-green eyes, cat-eyes. "They came to the states?"

"Some," he told her. "Some traveled to Africa, Australia, South America. We've lost contact with most of the factions. My great grandfather has insisted we try to locate the lost clans, but my father has had some success. People are too busy with their lives to seek out others. The ways of the past are vanishing, yet we are united."

She kissed him. It was a light kiss, a peck really, but she realized it was the first time she'd ever initiated anything sexual.

When the kiss stopped, she wanted to know more. "So...how did you come to be here?" She loved his story, his roots, his past and wished with all her heart she had the same thing, much had been lost to her.

"Alistair, yes, it was a shifter by the name of Alistair and he'd not found his woman and he became more desperate as time passed. The tales that were handed down spoke of a dream he had, one of the land across the ocean, America. He decided to travel to the United States in hopes of finding his soul mate.

"When 1831 rolled around, Alistair had convinced eight members of the Clan Chattan to emigrate with him. In the group there were six men, counting Alistair and two women."

Carr rose and walked to the tiny refrigerator, pulling out two beers. He popped the caps and handed one to Margo.

"It's a lot to take in." Margo sipped her drink. She wasn't sure what to say to Carr. "Your family, your history, makes me jealous."

"You'll find a family, be part of one." He spoke with sincerity and reverence.

She had a strange feeling he was trying to include her in his, but it wasn't going to happen. Jokul would find her and she'd run. "Are you trying to convince me of something?"

"I'll be honest with you, yes."

She changed the subject. "Is there more?"

"There's more to us and there's more story but what worries me is you. You're so closed up. You'd feel better if you talked about it. Your fears and why you can't share with me."

"Not happening." He was right. They both knew it but she didn't need to admit it. Feeling better and living to see the next day... When she thought of her daughter, she couldn't afford to be wrong about Carr McKenna.

"I'll respect your wishes for now." Yet he sighed as if defeated.

"Maybe I should go." She set the beer on the table and rose.

"No." He reached out to her, closing his hand around her wrist then tugging gently.

Uncertain what to do next, she sat down. "What then?"

"I'll finish what I started." He focused all his attention on her, his smile had vanished, dimples gone.

She nodded.

"The rogue clan settled in Texas. As time past and they found the right person to spend the rest of their lives with, they branched off into different directions. My clan settled in the Sierra Madres. Many of the clans mated with Mexicans and some of the Native American Tribes. All settled in isolated areas so there would be room to roam the land without discovery."

Tears nearly fell. The desolation and grief, she felt overwhelmed. She had traveled through time, jumped from country to country, and she had nothing like what Carr described. She'd never understood family until Sophie.

Family was so much more than one daughter. Even as the need to distance herself from Carr grew, the need for what he had spiraled exponentially.

"I'd like to paint you."

His voice brought her from her reverie. "What?"

"Naked."

~ * ~

"Yes, you'll be my model." The shocked expression on Margo's face intrigued him. He wasn't sure why she seemed surprised at his suggestion. She'd been willing to sleep with him.

"I've never done anything like that." She was shaking her head and shrinking into the couch.

He shrugged, trying for nonchalance. "There is a first for everything. I'm really a very good painter."

"Really."

"Really. Now let me see. While we had a few days off, I shopped for lingerie."

"Then I won't be butt naked." Her shoulders relaxed, and he nearly laughed outright before catching himself.

"For all practical purposes..." He held up a see through robe, lined with satin. It was purple, the color of royalty.

"Oh."

Once more, she was shaking her head. He sat down beside her and held her hands in his. "I'm not going to hurt you. I'm going to paint you. Let's say you can have the painting when it's finished."

"I just don't think this is a very good idea." Her breasts rose up and down, the agitation clear to see.

"We could make love." God, but he didn't want sex until he'd painted her. He'd thought this might give her a bit more time to adjust and to realize he had her back.

Suddenly her shoulders squared again. "All right, I can do this. What do you want me to do?"

"Take it slow for starters. Try to enjoy and be the beautiful model you are." His gut tightened. He didn't want her to be afraid of this but he needed to paint her, to explore every part of her with his eyes before he touched her.

"Is that all?"

"Well, no. See the table in the corner. That's where I'm going to have you pose. I'll draw lines where your body is supposed to rest so you can retrieve the exact same position when you take a break. It's grueling work to stay in one position, and you need to tell me when we need to stop. Do you understand?"

"Yes. What if I get cold or..."

"I've turned up the heat for this. This may take a couple of days so for now," he pulled her to her feet, "I want you to get undressed then into this. I've left a heavier bathrobe on the bed. You can wear that out and slip out of it when you're ready." He squeezed her hands. "This will all be good. You'll see."

"I'll be out in a minute."

While she was in the bedroom, Carr arranged the easel and adjusted the lighting around the table where he was going to put Margo. He wondered if he were a fool for doing this. Watching her naked, painting her, the thoughts made his body harden. He hadn't even seen her and he was ready for her.

She stood, framed in the doorway to his bedroom, a vision to him. Slowly, he walked to her and taking her hand, he led her to the table. "Take off the robe and sit down, I want your hands here and here, and I want you to face me. Position your legs this way."

Carr took the next few minutes to arrange her just the way he wanted her then reached behind her to loosen her hair and shake it out so it fell over her shoulders. He draped the see through robe so it framed one breast the other peaking out as if begging for his touch. Her legs were bent and seductively spread as she sat on one hip.

He tried to stifle the groan while he tried not to touch her. Touching her would be his undoing. With his eyes, he feasted upon her beauty.

He stepped back and crossed his arms over his chest, admiring his model and the provocative pose.

"What do I do now?"

"What? Oh, you stay in that position. Don't move a muscle." He wondered if he had the strength to see this through.

"Can I breathe?"

"Only slightly. You are going to be great, my sweet darlin'."

She nodded. He walked back to her and touched her chin, adjusting its position. Then he walked back to the canvass.

"I'm going to tell you what I'm doing every step of the way. I've set a timer for your break but tell me if you want to rest sooner. Don't nod."

She grinned.

Before I paint this with oil colors, I'm going in with a piece of charcoal to sketch you." He continued without speaking, outlining her basic form. The process was hell for him and he continued to wonder just what he'd been thinking.

The timer chimed, and he helped her from the table. She slipped on the other robe. "How am I doing?"

"You're perfection. You might want to stretch a bit. It will ease those muscles that don't like to stay in one position for such a long time."

She did as he told her. The break finished, she dropped the covering and positioned herself on the table. He made sure hands, feet, head and body were all where he wanted, then walked back to the easel.

"This time I'm going to fill in your main core."

He chuckled. Seducing her with his words was his first objective. He picked up the charcoal.

"I'm going to start here with the curve of your breast then the other—so soft." He drew while he watched her, and she watched him. "I'm tracing the aureole and now your nipple. It's growing hard, waiting for my lips to touch it, now the other. Can you feel my mouth on your nipple? Don't nod."

"Margo, I want to kiss you where the charcoal draws you. I'm drawing the length of your leg, kissing you with the touch on paper. Now back up to the juncture of your thighs. Are you wet for me? Do you want my lips there? Don't nod."

"Now, your belly button." He heard her groan and smiled, realizing he felt the same. Not only was he seducing her but he also seduced himself.

He was hot from the top of his head to the tips of his toes. He didn't think he could take much more of this. His hard cock rubbed against his jeans, begging to be set free.

"I need a break."

His body relaxed then tensed. He set the charcoal on the easel and strode to her. Scooping her into his arms he strode to the bedroom and kicked the door shut.

With a reverence he'd never felt before, he set her on the bed and came down on top of her, his arms on either side keeping his weight from her. Her delicacy always unnerved him. He didn't want to hurt her.

"I'm going to kiss you everywhere the charcoal touched the canvas.

"Carr... please."

He laughed. "You don't have to beg."

He bent close, kissed her forehead and trailed kisses across her face, her cheek, the tip of her nose, the other cheek. His lips touched her ear, his tongue swirling inside then he kissed his way down her neck, across her collarbone and treated her other ear to the same pleasure.

She moved beneath him, her hands rising to his chest. "Don't move," he whispered into her ear.

"But..."

"I'll explode if you touch me and I don't want any of this rushed. I need to go slow, take our time, reach a pinnacle we've never known before." Feathering kisses across her collarbone from one side to the other, he feasted on her, nipping, licking and kissing. His mouth traveled down the outside of her arm to her hand and her fingertip, sucking each one into his mouth and biting gently. He felt her body move against him.

Repeating the pattern, he traveled up the inside of her arm across her collarbone, back again to her other arm. Her hips bucked, touching him and he smiled, knowing she liked what he did.

"Your breasts are so beautiful." A moment passed before he kissed the underside of her breast, around the curve, giving it his full attention. Holding it in his hand, he moved to her nipple. The other nipple received his attention.

Sliding down her body, he continued with her belly button across the flat of her belly. Her hands wound into his hair, tugging while he traveled down the outside of her leg, still kissing nipping and licking.

God, but he'd never been so hot. Her toes were almost his undoing. Yet he continued and traveled up the inside of her leg, stopping momentarily at the back of her knees.

"Tell me where you want my kisses."

Silence followed then a groan of desire. He reached her pussy and laved the folds, touching her clit with his tongue. She bucked and shuddered with the passion he'd built inside her.

He gave his attention to her other leg and when he finished and he touched her swollen pussy again, she dripped cream.

"Enjoy." He pulled himself up her body and kissed her mouth. It was a deep long kiss, one that was meant to continue the seduction of

Margo. Their tongues battled, dueled. His finger found her nipple and rolled the hardened bud while her hips bucked. He knew what she needed, release. So did he, but he meant to prolong this.

Running his hand down the core of her body, he found her engorged clit and treated the swollen bud to his ministrations. She continued to buck and moan until she cried out and her body shuddered and convulsed.

He reached to his bed stand and grabbed a condom, unwrapping it with his teeth. Impatient to have it on so he could feel her body clench around his cock, he tore at the wrapper. Finally it was on and he was deep inside her. Her body responded wildly to him. With his hands beneath her butt, he raised her off the mattress and thrust, feeling her walls, feeling her unbridled response. He cried out and thrust once more, shuddering with the pleasure of his release while his voice mingled with her cries.

He rolled to her side, one hand cupping her breast. Her sweat-sheened body was so beautiful. If she stood by his side for his lifetime, he knew he'd never grow tired of her. She was his through eternity. Now all he had to do was convince her.

A few seconds passed, and her fingers were tracing his tattoo then down his arm and across his collarbone. He felt her kisses across his face, his cheeks, the tip of his nose and his ear.

God, but she was mimicking him. He didn't think he could withstand that but he sure as hell was going to try.

She started down his core, to his nipples, kissed and nibbled then sucked one into her mouth while the other she pinched with her hand. He swallowed hard and groaned. Her mouth found its way across his belly, and his cock came to life pulsing with need. But she bypassed it; her lips making wet marks down his leg to his feet then back to the apex of his thighs, before turning to the other leg.

He wound his hands in her hair and tried so hard to hang on to the little control he had left. His body shuddered then bucked.

He grasped her by the arms and pulled her up, then remembered the condom. Groping at the bedside drawer, he finally found one. In a few seconds, he had it on then he settled her on his cock.

"Ride me, my sweet misbehavin' darling'." He helped her at first. The rhythm between them so intense an inferno boiled within. He massaged her clit. Her climax came hard and fast. He cried out with her, and she fell onto his chest, her hair spread across his body.

"I can't move." She spoke softly as she traced the tattoo on his arm then seemed to notice the rosettes. "Are all of these tattoos? I never noticed them before."

"No, they are part of me. You see, golden jaguars have rosettes, black ones too but they aren't as apparent on the black jaguars as they are on the goldens."

"They're beautiful."

He watched her close her eyes. "Are you going to fall asleep?"

She shook her head. As she did, her hair shifted on him and the tiny movement inflamed him again. His cock throbbed with need for her.

Suddenly, she sat up, her nipples grazing his chest. "What time is it?"

"Hmm..." he reached for his cell to check on the time. "Five thirty."

"I have to get home." Her panicked voice brought him from his daydreaming.

"Shower first." He swept her into his arms and strode to the bathroom.

The shower was huge, made for two people as if the builders of the hotel knew what would happen here.

Still holding her in his arms and not wanting to let her go, he adjusted the water temperature with one hand. Steam filled the shower stall.

She was kissing his chest once more. He bent over, claiming her lips and opening them with his tongue. One more time, he'd make love to her, here in the shower before she left him.

Their tongues dueled. He adjusted her weight, "Wrap your legs around me." He felt her pussy against his belly, wet from the shower or cream from needing him? He wasn't sure and he sure as hell didn't care, because he'd have her ready for him. She responded so fast and so hungrily.

He braced her against the shower wall, holding her butt with one hand and exploring with the other. Bending over her and lowering his head, he sucked a nipple into his mouth.

Her fingers on his back, she held on to him, nails digging into his flesh.

He turned his attention to her other nipple and felt her arch her back to give him more room to suck the rounded breast deeper into his mouth.

She was slick and moist inside and ready for him. In a flash, he was deep and pushing hard. Overwhelmed at the moment, he felt her nails score his flesh and felt a strange sensation swirl around him.

She cried out, reaching her climax and he followed suit, but his body and mind twirled and his soul seemed to rise into the steam. He saw a vision of her body encompassed by his jaguar form. He closed his eyes then opened them and stared at the vision.

She clung to him, her nails still tight in his flesh. "What is that?"

Her query startled him, so immersed in watching what he was seeing. "I don't know." But he could guess and it wasn't the time to tell her.

As if time stood still, the two figures danced and mated and when they were done, they flowed into their bodies but not as he'd expected. The jaguar swept into hers and hers into his.

For the first time in his adult life he felt whole and at that moment he knew she'd become his mate.

Margo fell against him, her breath slow and even, her heartbeat seeming as one with his.

I didn't use a condom.

He had been told that a shifter could touch his mates belly and know if they'd conceived. Was it too soon?

His hand fell to her belly and he inhaled a sharp breath of air.

~ * ~

Margo pick up, please. He listened to the phone ring, not wanting to leave a voice message. Hearing her voice was what he needed. He strode down the steps of the plane.

"Hello?"

"Thank, God. I was worried about you. Where are you?"

"A... at home." She laughed but he didn't hear sincerity. "Checking up on me?"

"Not at all. I needed to tell you I left Tahoe. I'm at my great grandfather's ranch in the Sierra Madres. I'll be home tomorrow afternoon. Call if you need anything or if you see your stalker. I can fly home anytime. But Margo, this visit is important. I'll tell you more when I see you next." *I love you.*

The unspoken thought made him smile. He'd like to tell her sooner than later how he felt about her. She'd come over to his side. But first his curiosity had peaked and he had a strong hankerin' to understand what had transpired and the new sensations simmering inside. He'd never heard tell of anything that seemed to be happening within his core as well as his mind.

The airstrip was about a half mile from the ranch. He walked the distance in thought, trying to decide what he would tell his gramps. And what he couldn't.

Much of what had happened between Margo and himself was private, yet the swirling figures in the steam and the fact they switched bodies...

Well, he'd never heard of such a thing. Granted most shifters were private about their mating but this would have raised eyebrows.

The protective cloaking was another matter. He didn't know if that was what had happened, but every time he thought about Margo and feared for her safety, he felt an inner shift. In his mind he saw a cloak around her and it grew more dense with each thought. Then after this morning when the sex had been so complete and powerful, the cloak thickened again.

With the heel of his hand, he hit his head as if the gesture would clear his crazy ideas.

His gramps had his work cut out for him, explaining the experiences he was having. Gramps knew everything, his knowledge in the magical as well as the real world.

When he reached the ranch house, Gramps sat on the porch. He rose and held out his arms. They hugged then sat down. "I was expecting you."

Carr faced his great grandfather. "Gramps..."

But the old man held out his arms. "I sense you are coming within yourself. You are more than the second son, you must understand. Now tell me what has happened."

Carr's hands were clasped in front of him, his forearms resting on his legs. He stared at the floor. The time had come. He cleared his throat. "I've found my mate."

"This is good, my son, but there is more."

He nodded and looked at the man who had meant so much to the McKenna clan. He'd been there for them for so many years. Even after his mate died, he had not drowned in sorrow and despair.

"I'm not sure how much I can tell you. It feels so private, but the mating was like none other."

"It was magical?"

"Yes, but more than that." He moistened his lips. Carr went on to explain about the mating, and how their forms had left their bodies, swirling around in a silver mist then entered the other person."

When he finished telling the story, he felt exhausted, drained of all emotion. His gramps was sitting back on his chair, eyes closed and hands clasped in his lap. For a brief span of time, Carr wondered if he'd fallen asleep.

"Did she draw blood with both hands?" The words came out of nowhere, yet from his gramps.

"I don't know. I don't think so. We were in the shower."

"Take off your shirt and let me see your back."

Carr did as told then turned his back to the old man. He ran his fingers across his shoulder blades.

"Do you see anything?"

"Yes, there are two sets of deep scratches. She marked you and claimed you as her mate. Does she know it yet?"

Carr shook his head. "No and she would deny the fact. She doesn't trust anyone including me."

"Give her time." Gramps sat back, closing his eyes again.

Silence seemed to implode on Carr. "Can shifters cloak their mates and protect them from harm?" He drew in a deep breath.

"What makes you ask?" Gramps eyes were still closed, but Carr sensed he was fully alert.

"I feel it. Margo has a stalker and I've tried to protect her, but she won't let me. Then suddenly, when I was thinking of her, I sensed a coat of defensive something swirling around her. I don't know what it was. But neither of us has felt the stalker since I started sheltering her."

"Felt?"

"Yes, I feel a cold that hits me in the gut and can knock me to my feet. I don't think she has a typical stalker."

"No, she does not but she has to tell you what it is. You cannot save her until she trusts you."

"We're getting closer to trust. She's had problems in the past."

"Carr," Gramps straightened, his eyes solemn and his brows drawn together, "what you've told me is important to the clan. You are destined to greatness and your mate, she is not human is she?"

Carr started to respond, but Gramps held up his hand.

"Once every hundred years a shifter with your abilities is born. I sensed when you were just a child but had to wait until you grew to be an adult. You have become the leader of all the McKenna peoples. Your grandfather went in search of the Clan Chattan all over the world because he recognized that the time would come you would need their help."

"I don 't understand. Brody is the leader of the McKenna clan."

"True, but only the clan residing in the Sierra Madres, your immediate and close family members. You are the leader of all McKennas."

"How? I've always believed I had no responsibilities." He enjoyed acting the playboy and perhaps he was meant for something more important.

"That was a gift of your childhood. Now as an adult you have many priorities and you will be tested and challenged as time passes. You will also discover new abilities, ones besides cloaking. In time your strength and character will become apparent to all."

"Gramps, I'm not cut out to lead anyone."

Chapter Five

The '92 Datsun Jokul bought for Phaedra rolled into Tahoe with steam spouting from the hood. When the junk heap chugged to a stop, Phaedra swore under her breath. She turned the ignition and the car reluctantly started. A lakeside parking area was in front of her. She crossed her fingers, praying the car would get that far. She figured there was a time limit but she didn't care. Let them tow the damn thing away.

Once she parked, Phaedra rested her arms on the steering wheel before laying her forehead on her hands. When she'd protested this trip, he'd tightened her slave-collar. It was so tight now, she could barely breathe.

"Fuck him," she whispered to the air then shuddered as a wave of frost covered her body. Her fingernails were blue and she figured the rest of her was also freezing. Exhaustion swept through her, energy seemed nonexistent. Caring about herself or her future was no longer a viable emotion.

"All right, I'm sorry. Forgive me. I am going to find Atantsi if she's here." Phaedra pounded the steering wheel with her fist.

"She is." The gravelly voice came from inside her mind. For years she'd had no privacy from the ice demon. "She is close. I can feel it with every beat of my heart and hers."

Phaedra didn't want to listen to her thoughts or his. While she couldn't keep Jokul from invading her space, she learned she could sometimes keep her thoughts at bay, her mind empty. Leaving the car, her attention was on the lake and the way the sunlight rippled and danced. She sat down on a bench, hands clasped in her lap, breathing slowly and focusing on what she needed to do. Finding the hotel was first on her agenda.

A light breath of air passed by her. She turned to where she'd felt the breeze, but it wasn't Jokul. Nothing, but she felt a presence, a warmth she hadn't encountered for such a long time. Was it behind her?

She turned again and saw trees, people, park benches and cars in the parking lot. The lake was in front of her, the city to the other side.

"Was that her?" Jokul's enraged voice penetrated through her head. "Tell me now!"

"I didn't see anyone." She looked around once more. People congregated everywhere. "Atantsi is not here. I would recognize her if she was."

"Look again." The command was a threat and signaled eminent pain for her.

Phaedra rose and walked along the beach, shielding her eyes from the sun to see better. She walked for over an hour, searching for the young girl she'd sent into the future so many years ago. From afar she'd watched her grow up but she hadn't seen her since she fled Colorado a few weeks ago. The last time Atantsi had surfaced her hair color was different. She had red hair and this time...

Phaedra was sure the color would not be the same. Hungry and tired, she headed into town in search of her hotel. She'd memorized the name so she asked for directions and was soon outside the front door. But something stopped her from entering. Maybe she felt defiant, perhaps hopeful that events would play out different from the past.

She walked down the street, her attention on each building. A short time later, she stopped. She felt renewed, refreshed, optimism sweeping through her. She didn't understand her premonitions but this one felt right. Inhaling a deep breath, she stepped inside and walked to the front desk to register.

"Phaedra Wilson," she told the man.

"One moment please." He turned to the computer, and she watched fascinated as he typed on the keyboard. "That will be one hundred dollars a night. Cash or credit card?"

"Cash," she told him and handed him enough money to cover a couple of days stay.

"Room 409."

~ * ~

Margo's heart skipped a beat when she saw Phaedra strolling along the beach. She almost cried out to her but thought better of it. She knew Phaedra was controlled by Jokul and she couldn't' risk drawing her attention.

Phaedra wore a thin band of silver around her neck. The slave-collar meant that Phaedra would have no choice but to expose her to Jokul. Waves of despair and fear swept through her. She had hoped this time she would have a future, one she could share with Carr. With Phaedra at Tahoe, her presence jeopardized everything.

Walking quickly and keeping her head down, Margo followed a path leading away from Phaedra and into the woods. If she backtracked a couple of times, she'd reach Sophie's school as the buzzer blared. She could pick her up and head home.

She pulled out her cell and found Carr's name in her contacts. The phone rang, but he didn't pick up.

Trying not to sound panicked, her message was brief and to the point. "Carr, call me when you get this." Then placed the phone inside her pocket.

The school was about a half mile away. Still shaking from her near run-in with Phaedra, Margo arrived when the buzzer signaling the end of the day pierced the air. She waited for her daughter by the buses, and watched the children pile into the big yellow vehicles, and the drivers greeting each student.

"Mama." Margo turned to see Sophie waving and running toward her. "Mama, what are you doing here?"

"Hello, sweetheart." She scooped her into her arms and twirled her around, hugging her as tight as she could manage and trying not to let Sophie see her fear. "Can't a mother walk her child home? I've missed you so much."

"Why did you come? This is the first time." Sophie's expression turned serious. "You look sad, Mama."

My God, she was a perceptive little girl. Margo set her on the ground and took Sophie's hand in hers. "Because I couldn't wait to see you. Do you want to walk home with me or ride the bus?" Margo knew the answer or she wouldn't have asked. Even if Sophie rode the bus, Margo could take a few shortcuts and reach home before her little girl.

"I want to walk with you." Sophie held on to her hand.

Ten minutes later and in front of her door, Margo dug in her purse to find her keys. Pulling them out, she unlocked then opened the door. It felt good to be home with Sophie. She felt safe here even though she knew it would be short lived. She needed to make arrangements to leave. Where would she go this time? With no money, her options weren't looking good.

When they stepped inside the house, it smelled of vanilla and cinnamon, a scent Sophie loved. When they shopped together, Margo always let Sophie pick out one of those little cartridges you can plug into the wall.

"What do you want to do? Can you play with me?" Sophie tugged at her hand, which made her smile.

"Your choice, sweetheart." Unable to find her phone, Margo dumped the contents of her purse onto the coffee table in the middle of the room. A panic attack would not bode well. She didn't want Sophie to sense anything was wrong. God, but her little girl had been through too much in her short life. And now it was happening again.

Reassured to see the phone, she picked it up to see if Carr had read the voice message she'd left. "Damn." She couldn't figure out how to tell if he'd answered her. Frustrated, she set the damn thing back on the table.

"Mama..."

"Yes, where were we." Distracted she looked back to the phone as if thinking about it would make the little bells and whistles she'd programmed go off.

"We're going to play Barbies." She held one half-naked doll in the air. "Can you put this dress on her?"

Margo laughed, looking at her daughter and the favored doll. The clothes so small, they were kid proof. "Of course."

Sophie handed Barbie to her, and she struggled with the sleeves then the little snaps on the back. Shaking her head when she finally finished, she handed it to her. "There you are."

She'd received some money from Scott's pension when he died, but it wasn't very much. She managed to put enough away to rent a small U-Haul to drive from Colorado to Tahoe. Changing her name as well as her address meant no government agencies could find her.

And she prayed, neither could Jokul. But now that Phaedra had surfaced, she knew her time at Tahoe was limited.

She walked into the kitchen, cell phone in hand, and filled a kettle with water to make tea. The phone went off and she jumped.

Carr...

Looking at the screen, it read, *Can I come to your house?*

Her heart lodged in her throat. Was she ready to let him meet Sophie? But what choice did she have, sensing he was her protection from Jokul. *Let me think.* She texted back. She had to let him help because she didn't have the funds to move again.

Ok, but don't take too long. This is urgent and I don't think it will wait until your nanny gets there.

No pressure. She inhaled a deep breath. *Trust. This is a person you can trust. I hope.* In her mind there was always a little niggle of doubt.

God, but she did want to see him. She had spent most of the day thinking about him and yes, what he could do for her. She didn't like the self-serving mode, but she had to consider herself and Sophie first. Yet, in the back of her mind, she understood Sophie would be safer without her. Jokul didn't care about the child.

Hurry!!!! She texted.

The knock on the door startled her then sent her nerves into a spiral of fear. With shaking hands, she peeked through the window curtain.

"Carr, thank God you're here." She threw open the door. "Come in." Her agitated state could not be controlled. "You said it was urgent. I'm terrified of any news, yet need your help so much, I want to hear whatever you have to say."

He wrapped his arms around her, pulling her close as if to reassure. The kiss he gave her was quick and on her forehead. After what seemed like only seconds, he pulled away. "I think you should sit down."

"How did you get here so fast? You just texted me. I didn't know you were outside my door." She hugged him again then remembered

Sophie in the other room. Realizing her daughter watched, she forced herself to let go of him and stepped back.

"Mama? Is that the man you work with?" Sophie set the doll on an end table and stood, hands clasped in front her, a pensive look on her sweet face.

"I am. My name is Carr. What's your name?" He tapped her on the nose, grinning at her.

"I'm Sophie." Her voice sounded proud and happy.

Carr smiled at Margo. "Can you go to your room and play for a little while? Your mother and I have grown up things to discuss."

She nodded. "Yes, I'll take Barbie with me."

"You're such a good girl." Margo set her hand on Sophie's head. "I'll walk with you."

Margo returned to the living room with two cups of tea. "Didn't know if you like tea but it's all I have."

"It's fine." Carr sipped. "It's hot, wow."

"Sorry, just took the water off the burner." She fiddled with the teabag, dipping it into the hot liquid, and wondering where to start, from the beginning usually worked.

His eyebrows rose a fraction.

"I think—well." In truth she didn't know what information she could and couldn't trust him with.

"Thinking is good. Margo." He sat forward, arms resting on his thighs. "I know there is more to your story. I've learned a lot from my gramps but you have to fill in the details. You're magical and I'm guessing your stalker is too. I know you're in grave danger."

"Nail on the head." Heart pounding, she leaned back and closed her eyes for a moment. "Carr," she looked at him. "I'm so tired of running. Make it stop, please." She pleaded with him. She'd give anything save Sophie, to find a solution.

"I can't do that unless you start from the beginning and tell me everything." His voice was strong and sincere. He took her hands in his before bringing them to his lips for a reassuring kiss.

He seemed so patient. She began, "Like your clan, it was the time before-time. Only, I was born in that time. Our land was on top of towering cliffs in a western corner of Greece. It was called, Angizei ton Ourano. It means the land that touches the sky." She paused, watching for a reaction. He could stand, denounce her and walk from the room.

"Go on." His voice sounded calm and controlled, but in those few words she heard another emotion. Determination. "Tell me everything and understand that I believe you."

She swallowed hard. Dredging up the memories was hard but if he was determined, she could be too. "When I was six years old, my parents betrothed me to a man by the name of Jokul, and sent me and a later my servant girl Phaedra to live in his land of ice and snow."

"Why?"

Now he sounded angry. "To save our land. My parents ruled this country that touches the sky and he would have destroyed it."

"They could not have bargained for a few years before sending you away? Did they throw away a chance to bring up their daughter?"

"No. I don't believe so. I don't think he gave them a choice. Give me to him or see your country frozen was what my parents must have believed. Yet he destroyed the land anyway. In a rage he covered the land in ice." Tears formed, slipping down her cheeks. She wiped them away with the back of her hands.

"I've heard of this demon who cannot control his emotions. Yet he doesn't destroy entire countries. He usually coats the land in frost to show his power over the world."

"It was my fault, all my fault." Sobs threatened to choke her. Carr pulled her into his arms, the warmth of his caring embrace calming her shattered nerves. Yet she knew the rest of the story had to be told.

"No. This was not your fault. Never believe it. Jokul must take all the credit for his actions." His voice was sharp. He held her so he could look at her, putting a finger under her chin and lifting it. She blinked back the tears. "What another man does is not your fault."

"I caused it though."

"How?"

"I left him when I was sixteen." If she could do it all over, knowing what she knew now, she didn't think she would do anything different. She regretted all that had happened but...because of this she had Sophie.

"There was no reason to kill all of those people. Uncontrolled anger caused it, not you." His voice had gentled and he'd pulled her back into his arms, brushing the hair from her eyes.

She sat up straight, waiting for composure. Sipped her tea. "Yes, I am a firestarter but I didn't know how to use my power. He was a demon of ice and snow. Slowly he was destroying me. I had lived in his kingdom, gi apo pago kai chioni, the land of ice and snow for ten long years. Every year I grew weaker, my soul ebbing from my body. You see, he was not only covering me with frost, he was doing it from the inside out. I was slowly dying."

Carr's hands clenched tight, his expression grim. He stayed that way for a few seconds. "I wish I could have been there for you."

"Me too." Her smile wasn't genuine, didn't reach into her heart.

"How did you get away? He must have been confident you'd never leave." He didn't wait for an answer but rose and walked around the room, peering out the windows then checking on Sophie, who was absorbed in her play and talking to the dolls.

He must have known she needed time to think. When he sat down, she continued. "Phaedra helped me. What I didn't know until then was my parents had sent my servant with me for a reason. She had powers too. Phaedra is a seer and she gave me a crystal that would carry me through time."

"Did you get training for that too? I should have guessed as much when you told me you were born in the land before time."

"The instructions were quick and to the point. I had a few minutes to learn. I said goodbye and was gone. The first time I landed on an island in Greece called Santorini. It was no longer the time before-time. I don't know what year it was, I was too busy trying to stay hidden and survive. I lived there for a few years, made a few friends but he found me. Once again, I used the crystal."

"Until you ended up in Colorado."

"Yes, it was the boldest move and that's why it took Jokul so long. I lived there for seven years before he found me. I grew confident I was free of him."

"How old are you now? Well that's none of my business. Don't answer that."

She laughed, a small chuckle. "As in don't nod?"

"Something like that."

"I'm twenty-seven. How old are you?"

"Twenty-nine and I think I've absorbed enough information for now. Thank you." He kissed her on the nose.

"Why did you do that?" Sophie's little voice came from a spot behind her.

Margo felt as startled and sheepish as Carr looked.

"Because I like your mommy a lot."

"Mommy says you only kiss people you love. Do you love mommy?" Sophie's voice demanded an answer. Margo wondered what he would say.

"Do you want to sit on my lap?" Carr patted his legs as encouragement for the child.

Sophie cocked her head sideways then the other way. Her eyes narrowed to tiny little slits. "Ok." She clamored onto his lap, wrapping her arms around his neck. "Can I kiss you?"

"Thought you'd never ask."

Sophie kissed him on the cheek before leaning back and smiling at him.

Margo understood how quickly Sophie had fallen for Carr because she'd done the same.

"Sometimes adults kiss when they feel like it. Love doesn't have to be involved in any way. I just gave her a little kiss of affection because I do like your mother. And I like you too."

Her eyes narrowed even more. "I don't believe you."

~ * ~

Carr felt the laughter bubble up inside. He liked Sophie. She was honest and direct. He prayed she'd always have a wonderful life, and he meant to help her towards those ends.

He tapped her on the nose with his fingertip. "Are you hungry? It's almost dinner. What would you like?"

She didn't have to think. "Macaroni and cheese."

"Ah, a girl after my heart," he turned to Margo, "and you?"

"Did you have something in mind?"

"Thought we could order out. Do you like Chinese?" God, but he loved watching her. If he had his way, he'd spend every minute of the day either watching her or making love to her. Sex with Margo Cunningham was an adventure filled ride.

"Love it, but..."

"I'll call in the order and go pick it up while you make mac and cheese for Sophie." He paused. "Do you have a box of mac and cheese?" he asked as an afterthought.

She nodded.

"Good, I'll get a couple of movies too." Pulling out his cell, he made the call with Margo giving her input from the kitchen.

"You need anything at the store?" In the kitchen, he wrapped his arms around Margo, kissing the back of her neck while he hugged her tight. "I could use some milk. There's some change in the jar on the window."

"I'll be right back." He turned her around. This kiss was deep with tongue dueling. When he pushed away, he groaned. "You're going to have to come home with me tonight after we put Sophie to bed."

She pulled her lips together, shaking her head. "I can't leave Sophie."

"You do understand if Jokul is after you, Sophie is safer if you are not with her. Am I right?"

Margo sucked in a breath of air. "Probably, but it's so hard. What if..."

"The world is full of *what if's*, Margo. Second-guessing yourself, will not protect Sophie. You don't have to decide now, but promise me you'll consider what we've talked about."

He stepped out the door into the waning light of a sunny day. Looking up then down the street, he strode down the sidewalk. The grocery store wasn't far away. He needed time to think about everything Margo had told him as well as the knowledge he'd gained from his great grandfather.

He wasn't ready to believe he was a one-of-a-kind born once every century, a man who might have more supernatural powers than the ability to change his shape. He was just Carr. Once a playboy who loved to misbehave, now committed to his mate who didn't yet know she was his mate. He didn't believe he could lead anyone. Head of a clan was serious business.

Looking over his shoulder, he sent protective thoughts toward the house, Margo and Sophie. Again the sensation of power and magic swept through him. The belief he could protect them with a thought shouldn't be that hard to accept. But...

There was always a *but*, and he was sure this power didn't come without a price. What was that price?

As if on autopilot, he went through the motions, collecting his order at the restaurant then picking out two movies, one for Sophie and the other an adult flick.

When he reached Margo's home, Sophie was watching television and Margo was doing the dishes. The scene seemed so normal and homey, it near stole his breath. This was what he wanted for himself, reminding him of his childhood. Yet the feelings drove deeper into his soul, the normalcy of life was what he yearned for.

When she looked up and graced him with one of her beautiful smiles, he knew this was heaven.

"The plates are over there and the silverware in the drawer." She nodded her head in that direction.

After setting the sack of food on the counter, he turned toward her. "You don't want to eat out of the boxes and with the chopsticks?"

"All my food would end up on the floor. What do I owe you?" She wiped her hands on the apron she'd tied around her waist and reached for the jar where she kept the change. "I know you didn't take anything for the milk, and I'd like to pay half for dinner."

"It's on me." He couldn't let her pay even though he understood she didn't want to think of herself as a charity. She was his and he would pay for everything.

She sighed. "It's always on you. For once let me do something for Carr."

"Maybe another time." He liked the thought of her doing nice things for him. "You could give me a massage." He lifted an eyebrow, his dimples showing once more.

"You thinking naughty thoughts?" She put the pan she'd used for the mac and cheese in a cupboard. "It's not right that you pay for everything. I have the money now, thanks to you."

"I don't like this situation but I also don't like arguing about money. So I'll let it go." She wiped her hands on a dishtowel before picking up a plate and spooning food onto it.

They sat at the kitchen table, watching each other eat. Carr didn't know what to say to her. He wanted so much from her but he didn't' want to rush her. Patience had never been his strong suit.

"Marry me." Carr blurted out his feelings. "It's the only way I can keep you safe. You could be with me twenty-four hours a day."

"What?" She set the fork on the table and leaned forward.

"Marry me." Fuck, he sounded like a damn parrot.

"Be realistic, Carr, even married folk aren't together that much. I'd feel smothered."

"We can get married tomorrow." He wasn't going to let this go, knowing he could think of no other way to keep Jokul from finding her and taking her away from him.

"I don't think so." She swirled her food around on her plate.

"I'm sorry. I didn't mean to upset you." It really was the only way, and he knew he had to find the words to convince her. Maybe not tomorrow but soon, she would agree to become the newest member of the McKenna clan.

In the living room, he put Sophie's movie on the TV and sat back to watch. They couldn't talk, not during the show, but Carr knew she had questions and he had ones of his own.

A couple of hours later, Sophie was nestled against Carr's chest and on his other side, Margo's chin rested against his collarbone.

"I think Sophie's asleep."

"She is. What do you want me to do?" Carr enjoyed the pleasure of the little girl's trust. He would never waver and as long as he lived he would keep both girls safe.

"Let's put her to bed."

Carr swept her into his arms and strode into the bedroom with the precious bundle. Margo drew the covers back, and he set Sophie on the bed. He stepped back and watched Margo tuck her in.

"I love you, Mommy, and you too, Carr," Sophie whispered, eyes half closed then she turned over, pulling her teddy bear close and was asleep.

Carr draped an arm around Margo. They turned the light out and continued into the living room.

"I don't know if I should go with you." Her hands shook and tremors wracked her body. "I just don't know." Insecurities swept through her.

"I will shield the house and Sophie with my thoughts. I can keep her hidden and you as well. As long as I'm alive, I will not let anyone harm you or your little girl."

"How can you be so sure?"

"The same way you know Sophie is safer when you're not near here. Chalk it up to a gut feeling. But it's your decision."

Silence stretched between them. Carr cocked his head, waiting patiently.

"I'm thinking." Motherly, protective instincts had kicked into gear even though she knew Jokul wasn't interested in Sophie. "All right, I'll go." Her reluctance hit home but she understood in her heart her decision was solid.

"When will the nanny be here?" Carr was eager to reach his hotel. More discussion time with Margo was compulsory.

"I told her to come at nine. A half hour early, as usual." Margo laughed when she heard the doorbell.

Margo took care of the instructions for the night. "I'll be back by five AM."

~ * ~

"You take care of her now," Nanny said as she put Carr's cell number into her contacts. "And I'll make sure little Sophie stays just fine. If anything is the tiniest bit strange, I'll call."

"You promise." Margo's voice sounded shaky but she'd made her decision, and Carr believed it to be the right one.

In a few minutes, the pair were in the almost vacant hallway of the hotel. A waiter pushed a cart down the hall.

The nanny's words echoed in Carr's head when he heard Margo's sharp intake of air. His body tensed and all his cat-senses came to full-alert. If he had a tail right now, it would twitch.

"What is it," he whispered.

Margo moistened her lips, her eyes appeared filled with terror. "It's Phaedra, but she doesn't seem to recognize me."

Carr pulled her close and framing her head with his hands, he kissed her. The gesture blocked the view of the woman walking down the hall. Trying to see the lady while he lost himself in Margo, proved difficult. When she stepped into the room next to his, he stiffened.

"Did you see that?" The door closed to room 409. Carr grabbed Margo's hand and strode to his door, getting her inside as quickly as possible.

"She's here. Do you think she's knows about you, about me—us?" Margo stood at the balcony doors. "If I walked out there..." Hand shaking, she pointed to the balcony. "...she could be on the other side of the barrier."

The shudder he saw wracking her body terrified him. He just didn't know what was going on but he meant to find out. "You're not leaving here until I'm sure it's safe." He ran his hands thought his hair. "At least we know where she is."

"But if she is there," Margo pointed to the wall they shared. "Then Jokul knows I'm here."

"Not necessarily. Don't you think he would have done something if he knew?" Carr paused a moment, considering. "I cloaked the hotel. That means the entire building. Which..."

She didn't wait for Carr to finish his thoughts but jumped in with a question. "Yes, but what am I going to do?"

"We..." he corrected. "We're going to sit tight until I learn more about what I'm up against. So hold those thoughts." He pulled out his cell and put it on speaker.

"Hello."

"Dad, I need to ask something. Did Gramps tell you anything about our conversation?"

Carr felt the tension in the silence that followed his question. "He did."

"I need to call in reinforcements. Things are coming to a head here and it could be dangerous. Can you send Brody?" God, he wanted to ask for his entire family but he understood it would be too much.

"Brody is on his way. He decided to drive though so you won't see him until tomorrow. He has Lyn with him and if you need more, I can send the rest of the family."

"No, I think it will be fine. I just need to learn more about the demon." He paused for a moment. "I changed my mind. Send all of them."

"Son, he wasn't always bad. Remember, he has a purpose in this world as we know it."

"Really, tell that to Margo and her family. Tell that to Phaedra who he's kept as a slave. You can't possibly be implying we should save his life?"

"I'm not sure what I'm saying. Just keep my words in mind and if there is another way use it. Killing is not what we do."

"I'll remember your words, Father." He clicked off the phone and turned to Margo. "What do you think?"

"Is there another way?"

"Maybe, but I wouldn't trust Jokul to keep up his end of any bargain we might make. Once without honor always without honor, and I doubt if he is any different today than he was a few weeks ago or thousands of years past."

"Let's not speak of it again tonight." She wrapped her arms around him, laying her head on his chest. "I want to hear your heartbeat and feel the heat of your body next to mine and most of all I want you to whisk me away from the terror I feel every time Jokul's name is mentioned."

"Can I make you smile? Hmmm..." and forget your fear.

He pulled her close, holding her tight. His thoughts were free to roam and he had the gut instinct the cloaking of the hotel would also protect Phaedra.

"I just don't want to be tired any longer." She nestled in closer.

The heat of her body next to him was an aphrodisiac to his soul. "Let's go to bed."

She didn't answer. When he looked down at her, her eyes were closed, her breathing slow and even. Yet a lone tear lay on her cheek. He brushed it away and swept her from the couch. With Margo in his arms, he strode to the bed.

He started to undress her, unbuttoning her blouse.

"Carr?" She batted his hands away, her eyes opening. "What are you doing?"

He felt sheepish, chastised as if he were a child. Clearing his throat, he said, "I'm getting you ready to go to bed."

"Oh." Her lips formed an O. She reached toward him, and with her hands around his neck, she pulled him forward. "Make it all go away, at least for a few hours. Help me forget."

He needed to push her fears and her terror from her mind. Her hands were now beneath his shirt, pushing it upward and over his head. She felt so frail and delicate to his touch. Hell, she looked that way too. He helped her from her shirt then the rest of her clothes. He stood and slipped off all his clothes.

With wide eyes, she watched. "If you want, I'll just hold you, nothing else."

"I want to lose myself in you. Forget the fear. Can you do that?"

He'd die trying. "Yes," he choked out. Pushing away from Margo to look at her, with reverence, his gaze swept the length of her. She rested small hands on his chest. Slowly, he lowered to lay beside her. She snuggled close to him. He kissed her then, a long lingering kiss, meant to reassure rather than seduce. Until Jokul could be vanquished from the life she knew, Carr understood the fear would remain.

She responded, still, when his hands framed her face, he felt the moisture, the tears of fear she cried.

"Please don't be afraid," he whispered close to her ear. "Just feel what we have together." *I love you.*

He pulled back again, her hands framing his face. "I'll try."

"Good girl."

Margo's lips were still parted in surprise when Carr took her mouth. His tongue slipped between her teeth and he groaned when he tasted the minty flavor and sultry textures of her tongue. She made a small sound in response and lifted herself toward Carr's kiss, giving her mouth to him with a sensual need that made him ache once more to protect and shield her with his life.

Carr pushed deeper into Margo's sweet mouth, needing all of her, needing to soothe everything with their lovemaking all the way to his soul. The sounds she made deep in her throat, the desperate glide of her tongue against his, and arc of her body pressed against his erect cock, all told Carr that Margo needed the reassurance of life and the warmth of his body to comfort.

For a moment, Carr wondered if taking her here and now would assuage the fears. The distraction would be momentary but necessary. Her body's reactions told Carr that Margo wanted him the same way he wanted her; hot and wild, here and now, nothing but the driving rhythms of their bodies locked together in primal hunger...mercuric passion and flames twisting together, burning.

With a low cry, Carr tore his mouth free of Margo's, realizing that kissing her any more would mean there was no turning back. But for him, it was too late to stop the inferno consuming him. He was shaking, control slipping from his grasp one brutal heartbeat at a time.

"Fuck, Margo," Carr said roughly, muffling his voice against her neck. "Can we do this? Will it help you forget?"

"Nothing will help but I need you now. I want you again, before anything bad happens to me. I'm selfish."

"No, never that." His voice was raw and low.

Margo caught his tormented face between her hands and kissed him lightly. "I want to make it all go away too. But we both know that isn't going to happen tonight."

Carr shuddered, fighting for control. "Every time I look across the room and see your eyes watching me," his voice was low, uneven," I know what you're thinking, what you're remembering, what you're feeling. Your eyes are so full of fear, and I need to do everything in my power to take away the terror of Jokul."

"Hush," Margo murmured between tender kisses. "Tonight let's put our fears behind us. In the morning nothing will have changed but..."

Her words sent a bolt of fierce desire through him and dragged a raw sound from deep in his chest. He closed his eyes. "You're right. Nothing will have changed."

"I want you inside me now."

One of Carr's hands moved down Margo's body, caressing her breast and belly. Then he found her clit. It was the same as she was—hot, slick, hungry. He teased her until she cried out, her body coiling beneath his as precursors of passion swept through her.

Car's hand slid beneath Margo's hips, testing and caressing her flesh. Then his arm moved around her butt and he dragged her upward, lifting her, opening her to his attention.

He felt the sultry pulses of her desire embracing his tongue. The world darkened around him as passion coiled within, pulling him into Margo's hot center.

"Margo, look at me."

She opened her eyes. Carr was poised above her, his face dark with desire and his eyes like twin amber-green flames, burning.

"My sweet darlin', now."

With a smooth, powerful thrust, not stopping until their bodies were as deeply joined as it was possible for a man and a woman, he entered her.

Then he felt the secret, deep pulses within Margo. He drove into her and felt the sweet kisses of her climax licking over him, and pulled her hips tight against him.

~ * ~

Could Jokul be dead?

One could always hope, but Phaedra didn't think she could ever be that lucky. Still, her thoughts did not get a response from the demon. Her slave collar had not tightened. A frosty layer had not become a second skin.

I hope you never find her.

Nothing.

Touching the band around her neck, the circlet felt loose. When she tugged it flew off, her breath caught in her throat.

"I don't believe..." She bent over and touched the silver band, surprised the hated thing didn't jump back on her neck.

What was happening? She didn't understand any of this, which now seemed surreal.

The kissing couple in the hallway brought a smile to her heart. Some could find love.

Maybe she could too. *Don't let hope invade common sense.* Jokul had just lost focus for a time. He would be back and in her head. She dreaded the thought but knew it would happen. At least the slave collar was off and she didn't think he could put it on her from a distance.

Live in the present, and don't let the demon thoughts ruin these few moments.

She left the hotel, a spring in her step. On the street, a blinding pain struck her. "What have you done?"

Jokul's voice in her head left her shaking. "I did nothing. I don't know what you're talking about."

"You found a way to elude me. Where are you staying? And why didn't you go to the hotel I found for you?"

"I forgot the name."

Trying not to think of anything, she walked inside the hotel. His voice vanished. *Good God, he can't find me inside this hotel. If I don't go outside again, he might never find me.*

Can I live in the hotel forever?

Chapter Six

Life for her had turned full circle and for a short time she'd forgotten the sorrow as well as the fear. But now in the new morning light nothing was different. Smiling sadly at the thought, she pulled sheets around her and looked for Carr on the bed next to her.

Startled at the discovery he was missing, she sat up. He was humming in the shower. But the door to the bathroom opened and he walked out with a towel around his waist and wearing nothing else. The way he swaggered made her remember the night before, the sadness as well as the pleasure. At the moment, the lovemaking seemed bittersweet.

"I'm going to make all of your fears vanish and the sadness on your face turn to a smile. I promise." His easy grin and comment had her nodding her head in answer.

"I'm going to hold you to that, cowboy." She'd guessed the answer and for his sake tried to smile.

He sat down next to her. "I want to marry you today. Fuck that wasn't very romantic."

Kneeling on one knee, he slipped her hand in his. "Will you marry me? Today? Please." He seemed to hold his breath.

With the first announcement, she'd felt the blood flow from her face and with the second, she thought she'd faint, the bed beneath her whirling. "I promised myself I'd never take another husband." Her breaths came in short little pants.

"That bastard." He gritted out the words. "That bastard should burn in hell for what he did to you."

"He probably is." She pointed out, afraid of her feelings for Carr. She tried for flippant. "What's the rush? We hardly know each other."

His gaze went to the covers and slid up her body to her face. His dimples showing, he seemed to try for a new tact. "I've fuckin' kissed every part of you, my sweet darlin'. If that's not knowing you, I don't know what is."

"Fabulous sex doesn't make a marriage work." Margo felt his frustration and didn't know what to say. He was right though. Marriage to Carr McKenna would help keep her safe from Jokul. Her memories of the time she spent in Jokul's ice castle, clawed through her head. She'd never been welcomed by the demon or his men. A victim was how she'd thought of herself, when she learned the awful truth that her parents had sent her away to save their land.

"The danger is growing closer, and I can protect you better if we are husband and wife. You saw Phaedra last night and that means Jokul might not be very far behind. I'll tell you what," he paused.

"Don't bargain with me. I don't want to play any games." She withdrew her hand and set it on her lap. The thought of marrying Carr McKenna left her breathless. He would make a great father to Sophie and a good husband to her. Jokul would never be able to sway his loyalty. But...

Wasn't there always a but?

"When this is over, I'll give you a divorce if you want."

She inhaled a sharp breath of air. "Really?" Sarcasm bit at the word, anger flared and she turned her back on the man for a brief second. *A divorce if I want?*

"Did I say something wrong?" Carr sounded baffled, confused, and weary all at the same time.

"That was a strange marriage proposal and," she poked him in the chest, "I don't like surprises. Let me think about it."

"We don't have a lot of time. If Phaedra is next door, it's a matter of *when* not *if* she sees and recognizes you. Once she does, the ice demon stalker on your tail will blow frigid air down our necks."

"Do I have time for a shower before we leave?" She changed the subject but she didn't stop thinking about the proposal. Thoughts of Phaedra residing in the room next to hers terrified as well as intrigued. It seemed too big of a coincidence.

He nodded. "I'll order breakfast and it'll be here by the time you get out. Think about what I said."

And what he didn't say. Carr told her he'd protect her, keep her safe but he didn't say love. She'd always wanted to be loved. It had been so long since she'd felt her parents love for her. *Ok, girlfriend, don't get maudlin. It's time to be proactive and do what you need to do for Sophie's sake. This is no longer about you.*

By the time she stepped into the hot water and let the heat warm her body, she'd made up her mind. She would marry Carr McKenna. Even though he didn't love her, he was a good man, a caring man.

Weren't those sentiments the same for her first marriage? She recalled how that had turned out.

What more could she want or need? If she let him slip a ring on her finger, she wasn't going to end the marriage. She was in it for keeps. Sophie needed a father.

In the living room a table had been wheeled in with what appeared to be a four-course breakfast. The aroma of bacon and hash browns filled the room.

"Who's going to eat all this?" She had to laugh at the sheepish expression on Carr's face.

"You and me."

"I," she began. "I'll give it my best."

He pulled out a chair for her to sit down. When he uncovered all the plates, not only had he ordered bacon and hash browns, but there were eggs and sausage, waffles and pancakes and berries.

She looked at him in wonder. "Did you order everything on the menu?"

He shrugged broad shoulders, giving her a wink at the same time. "I didn't know what you liked. You can take something home to Sophie."

She nodded and helped herself to a plate before sitting down. "I've been wondering." She was getting used to his overbearing but sweet generosity.

"About what?"

She wasn't sure where she was going with this or how possible. "Do you think I could see Phaedra?"

"No."

His quick response surprised her. She'd thought he might think about it, for a second. "Why not?"

"You need to ask?" He'd put down his fork and was staring at her. "You can't afford to do anything foolish."

Tears welled in her eyes and she brushed them off her cheeks with the back of her hands. "It's been so long. I loved her and she's my only tie with my parents."

"Maybe when this is over."

"You really believe it will end? He will never give up and I was thinking, if you can protect me, couldn't you do the same for Phaedra?"

He took her hands in his. They were warm and his touch filled her with feelings of confidence. He was her refuge, her safety. She wanted that for her girlhood friend.

"I don't know. Ask yourself, is it worth the risk?"

Was it worth the risk?

"Yes." She didn't need to think about it. "Could I live with myself if we didn't try to save her? The answer to that question is, no. You have the ability to shield me from him, couldn't you do the same for my friend?" she repeated.

He poured syrup over his pancakes. "I don't know. I was thinking about it last night. And I wondered too, if perhaps the fact you were shielded here in the hotel she would be also. Maybe Jokul has no more control over her."

"Could you try?"

"I have and I believe she is protected as long as she is in this hotel. If she leaves though, I don't think I can keep him away from her. I've just learned of my ability to cloak things and people. I'm stretched thin."

"I see."

"Fuck." For a moment his dimples showed. "You're up to something."

"Could you knock on her door? Talk to her." She was terrified of what he might find out, yet eager to know.

"When?"

She smiled at him but said nothing.

"If you put it that way." He set his napkin on the table and rose. "When do you need to be home?"

"I'll call Nanny and explain to her that we'll be a bit late. I'm sure it will be fine with her. She always tells me to do whatever I need to do and to take as much time as I want. She loves Sophie and enjoys the time with her."

"Wish me luck," he sighed as she saw him leave. Lord, but she wished she could be a fly on the wall.

Time ticked by so slow. She paced, back and forth, back and forth. Her cell had ticked off one minute and it seemed like an eternity. At the door, she wanted to open it and follow Carr to Phaedra's room.

Her stomach rolled, her hands sweating. She rubbed them together and wiped them on her skirt.

The door opened and she saw her.

"Atantsi? Is it really you?" Phaedra ran to her, arms wide.

The hug was filled with love and sorrow for the lost years. "Are you," she stopped. "The collar, it's gone."

Phaedra stepped back. They were at arm's length, both studying each other. "It's the hotel. I'm protected here. I discovered the truth yesterday when I left. I hadn't heard from Jokul but when I stepped outside, his voice flashed in my head. He is still filled with hatred."

"But the collar."

When I hadn't heard from him in so long, it loosened and I was able to take it off. I burned it. But when I discovered I couldn't hear from him, inside this building, I decided I couldn't leave."

"I can protect her as long as she is with you," Carr said.

This couldn't be better. "You can be our witness."

"Witness to what?" Carr stepped up beside Margo and draped an arm around her.

"I've decided to accept your proposal." God, her heart thundered in her ears while her world tilted upside down. She'd never thought to marry again. "Sophie needs a father."

"You don't have any feelings for me?" His grin faded into a blank stare.

"Of course I do." She didn't know how to tell him how much she'd come to rely on him. Despite her need to be independent, she liked the way he did things for her, how he thought of her.

"Enough about this. We will get married. I'll make the arrangements. You and Phaedra finish breakfast." He motioned to the table. "There's enough food to feed an army."

"Thanks, I am hungry." Phaedra sat at the table, helping herself.

Margo boxed up food for Sophie. Carr had even thought of boxes when he ordered.

"You two chat girl stuff. I'll be back in an hour."

"Promise?" She did need to get home. She pulled her cell from her purse and called Nanny. "I'll be home in about an hour. Is that okay with you?" Shifting the phone to her other ear, she said, "Good, I'll see you then."

"Will I get to meet Sophie?" Phaedra had stopped eating, her eyes imploring.

Margo saw the pain in her expression, understanding it would take a long time to get rid of her horrible memories. "Yes, Sophie will love you just as I do."

"I'm sorry but I had to tell him about Scott. He used the slave collar to control me. I never had a moment alone. He was inside my head all of the time. Once I saw you, he always knew, until now. It's Carr isn't it? He protects you somehow."

She felt so sorry for her but Margo wasn't sure how much to tell her friend. As much as she didn't want to think about it, this could be a trap.

Phaedra gave her what looked to be a half-hearted smile. She set her fork down. "You don't trust me."

"Honestly? I want to, it's just that..."

"If he figures how to get back inside my head, he'll know where you are. Don't think I haven't thought of that."

She jumped, startled by the door opening. Carr stepped inside, loaded down with packages.

"I bought something for you and you." He nodded his head first at Margo then Phaedra.

"For me?" she sounded incredulous. "I don't remember a time anyone has given me a gift."

Margo rose and helped him with the packages, thinking of the life her friend had lived. "Really, Carr, you do too much."

He grinned full out, his dimples showing. "Never. I love giving you things and watching your eyes light up with pleasure."

For the last week, Margo felt like a little kid in a candy store. She opened the package he handed her and pulled out a simple white gown. "It's beautiful."

"I hope it fits." Carr rummaged in the bag. Now on one knee, he opened the little black box. "Will you marry me?"

Confused by his question, she told him, "I said, yes."

"But it wasn't official. Now it is." And he held her hand in his and slipped the ring on her finger.

"This isn't simple."

"Yes it is. It's a solitaire and they don't come more unpretentious. It's just big. Do you like it?"

"You've got that right." She held up her hand, admiring the rock.

"Do you like it?

She didn't think she'd ever heard him sound so unsure of himself. "I love it." After her initial reaction, reassuring him was at the top of her list.

"Well, good, you guys go try on your dresses. If they don't fit or you don't like them, we can stop in the hotel store and find something else.

~ * ~

Carr paced the living room, waiting for the girls to emerge. He heard their chatter and was pleased by their reactions to his gifts. He'd been relieved when Margo accepted the dress and the ring. The last thing he wanted was for her to feel as if he'd bought and paid for her.

His brothers and sisters would be in Tahoe in a few hours ready to witness his marriage and defend his wife. His dad had called him while he was out to tell him everyone was coming.

For some reason he didn't like thinking of her as his mate. Yes, she was his soul mate but no, she was much more. Mate was a word that didn't sound human. He shook off the notion, understanding that was what his clan called their women. His mind went back and forth with the thoughts.

Startled from his musing by the sound of Margo's voice, he looked up.

"They fit perfectly. You've a good eye for size." Margo had the dress draped over one arm as did Phaedra.

"You're not going to show me?" Disappointed he strode to her and kissed her, draping his arm around her. "We need to get going and test my cloaking abilities. I'm not sure what will happen once we're outside the hotel."

"It's bad luck for the groom to see the bride in her dress before the wedding." Phaedra picked up Margo's gown. "I'm going to make sure everything goes as planned. And I believe your abilities to shield us will work fine. We're, after all, much smaller than the hotel. Should be easy for you."

"God, I hope you're right." If anything went wrong, well he didn't want to think about it. He did know he'd defend Margo first.

"Do you have the wedding rings too?"

"In that bag." He picked it up. I'm going to have Brody be my best man. They're meeting us at your house. "I found a dress for Sophie too. I'm guessing you'll want her to be your flower girl."

"Is all this necessary. I thought we'd just go to the justice of the peace."

"I did that too. I have the papers and all they need is your signature." He handed her the papers.

Margo pursed her lips. "I don't know how to write in English and my name..."

"Your name? Margo isn't your real name." He should have known, should have asked before he had the papers drawn.

"I'm going to have to use my name from my marriage to Scott." She turned to Phaedra as if silently imploring her to tell her what to do.

"I think that would be fine. If I'm remembering correctly, your last name was Cunningham."

"Yes. It was but the documents were left in Colorado. When I fled, all I had time for was to pack a bag of clothes and drive. I was so afraid and in such a hurry." She signed the documents with Carr's help.

"Let's go get Sophie and wait for my family. They should arrive in about an hour." Carr grabbed the packages and opened the door for the girls.

The drive seemed to pass quickly. They talked about the plans, keeping everything as simple as possible.

"Mama." Sophie met them at the door, jumping into her arms and giving her a huge hug and kiss.

"I love you, sweet pea." Margo twirled her around and around.

I want that, a little girl to love.

"Sophie, we've something to tell you." Margo set the child down then led her to the couch where they both sat.

She looked at her mother with huge brown eyes. Carr wondered what was transpiring in her head. Was she worried about what Margo was going to tell her?

Would she be happy with her mother's decision to marry him?

Margo inhaled a deep breath of air, waiting for a moment. "Sophie, Carr and I are going to get married today and if you want you can be the flower girl."

Sophie's expression was one of puzzlement. Carr thought to laugh but held the chuckle back.

"I don't know." She looked down then back to her mother. "What would I have to do?"

Phaedra pulled the flower girl dress from one of the bags and handed it to Margo. "First you would get to wear this really pretty dress."

Sophie's eyes grew big, lighting up at the same time. "It's pretty, Mama, and it's my favorite color, pink."

"Carr picked it out."

She looked at him, and he nodded, pleased Sophie liked his choice. He stuffed his hand in his pockets, rocking back on his heels as he watched the two of them.

"When we get married, you can hold my hand and walk down the aisle with me."

"Is Carr going to live with us?"

"Yes, yes he is."

"Can I put it on right now?" She jumped from the couch. Tugging on Margo's hand, she headed for her bedroom.

Carr's cell rang. "Go on, it's Brody. He says they are here. Guess he parked down the block a ways."

"What now?" Margo stopped at the door to the bedroom.

"I'll go meet them."

Carr stepped outside. Shielding his eyes from the glare of the sun, he watched his siblings stride down the sidewalk. They were an imposing sight.

Brody led the way and walking behind him were the twins, Lyn and Kimi. Between the two girls strode Guy. His heart caught in his throat. Angel McKenna strode behind his siblings.

Had he really been jealous of Sophie's love for Margo? He consoled himself with the thought that his jealousy had been momentary. His family was with him now, willing to put their lives on the line to help a woman they didn't know. His family loved him unconditionally.

Lyn broke ranks first, dashing down the sidewalk to give him a hug, wrapping her arms around him, she whispered, "It's all going to be okay. We're here and we won't let anything happen to your mate."

Carr was struck with the memory of Lyn's almost lifeless body when she'd battled the Amazonian devil for Sadie. He'd carried her down the hill to the medicine hut and he'd stayed with her until she woke.

She stepped back and gave the others room for hugs and slaps on the back.

"You promise me, all of you, that you'll be careful." Lyn stood with her hands on her hips and feet planted.

"Of course," they said in unison.

Carr knew what that meant. They would move heaven and hell and worry about their own safety after the mission was accomplished.

"Let's meet your wife to be." Brody led the pack to the doorstep but before opening the door, he waited for Carr. "Don't want to barge in unannounced."

"They know you're all here." Carr opened the door.

"Welcome." Margo stepped into the room, and Phaedra stood at the back of the living area. "Sophie is admiring herself in her new dress."

Carr made the introductions and the awkward moment seemed to stretch into eternity.

"Drinks anyone?" Margo asked.

"We should be going to the chapel. What do you need?" Carr hugged her and whispered close to her ear, "Do you like them?"

"Just my dress. And yes, I think so. I don't know them."

"Is there a place to change at the chapel?" Phaedra asked. "Don't want the groom seeing the bride too soon. Bad luck and all."

"We have two cars. I'll drive Margo's, and Brody, you take Carr and Guy with you. Kimi and I will go with the girls."

"I'll go with Guy, Brody and Angel. We'll meet you there." Phaedra smiled. "This is the happiest day of my life. I wanted to see you happy and to be with you."

~ * ~

The venue looked over Lake Tahoe and sunlight rippled across the water. Brody had taken charge and rented tuxes for the men, and the twins had bought lavender dresses.

Carr had never been as nervous as he was at this moment. He waited at the head of a deck overlooking the lake. He prayed his newfound cloaking skills would get them through the ceremony, their whereabouts still unknown.

He had taken a huge chance riding in a separate car from Margo, but they'd stayed close and nothing seemed to be amiss. Now he waited for the ceremony to begin and Margo to make her entrance. Brody would be his best man and Phaedra would give Margo away.

Music began to play. His attention turned to the entrance and he stiffened, his hands trembling.

Brody whispered, "Got the ring, little bro?"

Carr nodded and slipped his hand in his pocket to check. The box was there.

"You nervous?" This time Brody's question seemed sincere.

Again Carr nodded, watching the entrance, thinking about the protection he was supposed to give the girls.

He tightened his fists as a cold chill washed over him. This damn lake was too open. He needed this over. Yesterday.

Sophie walked down the aisle, tossing petals as she approached them. She smiled at him, and the sight melted his heart. He had an instant family. Two weeks ago, he would have never believed it if someone had told him he would be getting married today.

Margo stood at the entrance, a bouquet in hand. She looked amazing, beautiful. The moment was one he intended to keep close to his heart through all eternity.

The ceremony didn't take long. Before he could reflect on the words and their meaning, he was kissing his bride. He wanted so much more, needed her love.

He gave her a quick hug before turning to the most important people in his life. Raising his hands, he announced, "We're married."

Laughter rang out around them as they walked across the dock to a horse and carriage. Three horse-drawn vehicles waited to carry them somewhere. "What?" he asked, surprised by the sight.

"Dinner and champagne," Lyn said. "Brody helped arrange it."

"We're going to celebrate until midnight." Kimi laughed. “This is something we never thought would happen to our playboy bro.”

"What are you waiting for? Get in," Brody said as he climbed into one of the carriages, the others following suit.

Carr had to admit it was romantic and he'd bet his last dollar Sadie arranged this. She wasn't here but her stamp was on the starry-eyed carriage ride and what would be a romantic dinner.

He kissed Margo again. "I think Sadie has done this. Lyn is not a romantic, and Kim is too shy. What do you think?"

"Either that or Phaedra."

Carr pulled Margo into his arms. Closing his eyes, he sent a wave of emotions showering his friends and family. He'd felt a moment's cold when he'd been on the dock waiting for Margo. Focusing on Margo and Phaedra, he prayed he hadn't let them down.

~ * ~

Jokul stood atop the icy turret that was his home, waiting for news. He'd sent his men to Lake Tahoe and surrounding area searching for both Phaedra and Margo.

"Sir, your men are back." The servant bowed out after giving Jokul the news.

His fists tightened. He'd told them not to return until they found the two women. If they'd found Phaedra, he'd be inside her head.

"Where are they," he growled when the men entered. "I told you I didn't want to see your ugly faces until you found them."

"I almost lost my life. A wolf and four huge jaguars battled us in the woods where we'd made camp." The man's voice quavered.

Jokul stepped down from his viewpoint and approached his servant. His fury simmered inside, ready to explode. He waved his arm with violent motions. "Perhaps you should have fought to the death. It would have been more honorable."

The man cowered. "My lord, Jokul..."

Shaking, Jokul pointed at the leader of his men. Ice flowed from his hand onto the man who froze midstride. He shattered, his body exploding into tiny pieces, clattering onto the floor.

"Find them!" Jokul roared, spittle flying from his lips.

The three remaining men backed from the room. Jokul strode to the door and slammed it shut.

"Incompetence. I'm surrounded by inept fools." He walked to the terrace and looked over this frozen land. He'd had plans for both Phaedra and Margo. How the fuck had she eluded him for so many years?

Phaedra must have helped her. Even with the tightened slave collar, the woman knew he wouldn't kill her. He needed her. She'd been able to withstand what he knew to be excruciating pain and now this.

Her loyalty to Margo was something he couldn't believe. But there it was right in front of him.

He'd sent Phaedra to Tahoe and she'd disappeared. The impossible had occurred and now what the devil was he dealing with? Wolves and jaguars?

Even though he felt sure it was futile, he tried to hear Phaedra's thoughts. Focusing all of his energy in her direction, he stood as if frozen.

He heard her laughter then the window snapped shut.

Chapter Seven

Carr had reserved the small banquet room off the large dining area in the restaurant earlier in the day. A crystal chandelier that hung in the center of the room radiated sparkles of light. The scent of baked bread and perfectly cooked prime rib filled the area where the wedding party ate.

"My stomach is still rolling. I was so afraid Jokul would sweep down and freeze everyone." Margo played with the food on her plate before looking at Carr. "This isn't going to end any time soon is it?" Her heart in her throat, she needed to hear a promise from Carr but it was one she knew he couldn't give.

"Jokul is in your past. I promise you this. If he harms you or even frightens you again, I will end him." Carr gritted out the last words, his hand tightening around his fork before jabbing the meat he'd just cut.

His words frightened her more than her fears. "I don't want you to act on your emotions and do something foolish." She paused, gazing around the room, trying to find the happiness she was supposed to feel on her wedding day. "Look, Phaedra and Angel seem to like each other." Margo nodded at another table where the pair looked to be in serious conversation. "You said he's related to you, how?"

Carr laughed, "He's a cousin but I don't know how far removed. Funny thing is, he's a shifter too, changes to a wolf."

"You're confusing me." She didn't see how that was possible. "I guess anything is conceivable. How does that work?"

Carr shook his head, his sexy dimples showing when he grinned. "Don't know. Last year when he showed up, hunting the Amazonian devil and after he introduced himself, told us the gene mutated."

She set her fork down and started to speak but found she was speechless. A mutated gene and his part of the clan changed to wolves not big cats. That was a lot to take in at the moment.

"Is that all you're going to eat?" Carr reached over and swiped a roll off her plate then spread it with butter. "You need your energy for the night to come. I've plans, my sweet misbehavin' darling."

"Yes." She blinked a couple of times, wondering if he meant to change the subject or if he was still hungry and didn't want to think about Angel McKenna. She wanted to tell him the only one misbehavin' was Carr McKenna. But she blushed when she thought of the things she'd done with him.

"So..." She paused, trying to form the words and wondering if he wanted children. "If we had children..." Would they be shapeshifters too?

"We will." He plopped half the buttered roll in his mouth. "It's written in the stars. I bet if you asked your friend Phaedra, she could tell you how many and the sex of each one."

"You seem pretty sure of yourself." She realized she did want children with him. While her future seemed brighter it was far from secure. Children should come later not sooner.

"I am very sure. We will have as many as you want." He ate the other half of the bread.

"If we have children," she began again then held up her hand to keep him from diverting her question again. The question that wouldn't go away. "Will they be shapeshifters?"

"Of course." He helped himself to more bread, this time from the breadbasket instead of her plate.

"And you know this how?" She didn't understand how he could make such a positive statement.

Carr paused in thought. "It seems as if all the children are shapeshifters. Never heard of one that wasn't, but I suppose anything can happen." He stopped speaking again. "Will they be firestarters too?" His dimples appeared for a moment.

"That's frightening. A child who could change shape and start fires was a crazy notion. And I have no idea. This goes beyond any knowledge I was granted. You remember they sent me away when I was very young."

"We'll just have to wait and see." Carr laughed, shrugging his shoulders. "It's kind of like waiting until the child's born to see if it's a boy or a girl." He gave her a quick kiss.

"Not exactly." A huge responsibility had just been thrust on her, on them. "How do you bring up a child with magical abilities?"

"Very carefully." His solemn voice resonated within. "My sweet darlin', damn cautiously."

She gulped down her glass of champagne. He poured her another one. Wanting to down this drink too, she changed her mind, pushing the crystal away.

"I'm taking this seriously. You know how easy it would be to abuse the gifts granted at birth. The child will have to understand what he can do and respect that power."

"I understand. It's a good thing you married someone as strange as you." Carr laughed again. "You know I'm joking, right?"

"Yes, but what you say is so close to the truth it's not really funny and makes me pause." She thought about Sophie and wondered if the child was a firestarter. She didn't think her little girl had powers. She hadn't shown any abilities towards that end. No fires in the garbage cans or anything else. But Sophie didn't anger easily. She was so calm most of the time it frightened her. Then Carr asked the question that was on her mind.

"What about Sophie?" Sophie sat with Nanny at a nearby table. The two had made up some kind of game, and the little girl was laughing at Nanny's antics.

"I don't know yet. I'll ask Phaedra if she has any ideas about it. Phaedra knows a lot more than I do." The woman had taught her what little she knew, and Margo prayed she'd stay and help her with Sophie.

"You should do that, ask Phaedra. Sophie will need to be taught. I hope Phaedra doesn't have any plans of leaving."

Margo looked to the opposite table. Angel held both Phaedra's hands in his.

"She has to stay until Jokul is convinced I'm no longer his. She was held prisoner. I hope she doesn't venture anywhere without help."

"Angel may have something else to say about that." Carr focused on the couple. Margo thought the pair was at odds with what she remembered about Phaedra, but she knew next to nothing about Angel.

She watched as Angel kissed the back of her friend's hands then the palms. "They look pretty serious. I wonder what they're saying to each other."

"They've only met. It could be a crush or a need to feel wanted. I think Angel has always been a loner." Carr rose from the table. "It's time for us to get back to the hotel. Brody will take Sophie home and the siblings will stay there. It's up to Nanny whether she wants to go or stay."

The decisions were made. Lyn and Kimi would go with Sophie, and Nanny would stay at the house too. Carr and Margo would spend their wedding night in Carr's hotel room. Brody booked a nearby room, and Angel would stay with Phaedra.

At the hotel, the foursome stopped at the bar for another round of drinks. Margo needed to speak with her friend about jumping into a relationship without thought. She didn't think Phaedra had much experience when it came to love.

Like what I did.

"I'll be right back. Come with me, please?" Margo directed her question to Phaedra.

"A little girl talk?" Phaedra asked with a small laugh. "I know what you're going to say."

Margo nodded. "Do you? I'm not sure I know what I'm going to say. I certainly can give my opinion but as to advice, I have none."

They walked silently to the ladies' room. Margo's mind raced with thoughts and ideas, but if Phaedra was really falling in love with Angel then who was she to say back off? Phaedra deserved happiness as much or more than anyone. If Angel was the one who could chase her sadness and loneliness away, then she should give the relationship a try.

They sat in the sitting room on the lounge chairs. The walls were papered in a mauve flower design and the chairs were wicker and draped with a vanilla-colored fabric. A floral scent permeated the room.

Margo spread her gown around her legs and feet. With a huge sigh, she said, "I'm ready to get into something more comfortable."

"You look beautiful and I'm sure Carr is ready to get you out of that dress too." Phaedra laughed and winked.

"I won't argue with that." Margo decided on a direct route to her questions. "Do you like Angel?"

"Of course I do. What kind of question is that?" Phaedra pulled back her hair, letting it fall down her back.

"It's the kind of question a friend asks. I don't want to see you hurt and Carr says Angel is a loner."

"Honey," Phaedra leaned forward, "I'm not looking for a long term relationship. I've been abused and threatened by a man for so long." She paused. "Angel makes me laugh and I don't remember the last time I felt joy in my heart or heard the sound of my own damn laughter."

"I'm sorry. It was my fault. You helped me leave and suffered the consequences for your actions."

"Don't lay a guilt trip at your door. It's Jokul who is at fault not anyone else. He's evil and has to be stopped. And remember, we both got away from him."

"With Carr's help."

"Yes, and honey, you need to focus on making your bridegroom happy tonight. Forget about me. You need to think about yourself first."

"I'll try. But you and I both know there is going to be a confrontation of some sort. Why do you think he rallied the troops, his siblings and his cousin. He called in the big guns too. I think his father has approached others of the Clan Chattan and called in their assistance too."

Phaedra looked as if she wanted to say something then closed her mouth. Margo waited, thinking.

Then she said, "I'm speechless. More is going on here than I can understand."

"He's told me some things about his family but there is so much more I don't know. They go back in time as far as mine." Margo paused, inadvertently smoothing the folds of her gown. "But his lineage survived. Mine didn't."

"You look sad and that shouldn't be, not on your wedding day."

"I'm afraid, terrified really. I don't want anything to happen to Carr or his siblings, not on my account."

"Do you love him?" Phaedra leaned forward, waiting for her to answer.

A long silence followed. Did she love Carr? With Scott the answer had been easy. Scott had been a friend and a confidant. She had never loved Scott.

"I don't know what love is or how it feels."

"You love Sophie? Right?"

Margo knew that kind of love was different. But was it really so different? How were the feelings of love for a child the same as the emotions when they involved a man?

"It's different, Phaedra. I would give my life for Sophie, protect her with all my heart and soul. She is of my blood and will always be my daughter. No one can ever take that away from me."

"Margo, would you protect Carr with your life?"

Of course she would, but Carr didn't need protecting. "Yes, I don't think he would let me."

"Whether he would allow it doesn't matter, the feeling is in your heart."

This was all too much to think about right now. She wasn't ready to give Carr words of love. "I can't tell him I love him. Not right now."

"Did you marry him for his protection?"

"Yes and no. He's damn persuasive." And he had been. With so little time to think about any of this, they'd rushed the wedding day. To Margo it seemed Carr wanted to wed her as soon as possible. Yesterday wouldn't have been soon enough for him.

"If your life hadn't been threatened by Jokul, would you have married him today? Take your time, think about the question."

"No, but it doesn't mean I wouldn't have married him." This wasn't going so well. She'd brought Phaedra into the powder room to talk about Angel and somehow the conversation had turned to her.

"Then you don't love him?"

"I didn't say that."

~ * ~

Carr stretched his legs out, leaning back in the chair. He'd ordered drinks, and Angel had done the same.

"Don't hurt Phaedra." Carr studied the man who had come to his family's assistance a little over a year ago. "She's a beautiful woman who's been through hell for many years. Don't hurt her."

Angel didn't respond to Carr's idle threat. His voice grim, he replied, "We have other things to speak of."

"Not to me but I'll listen." Carr didn't know what Angel was about to say, but he was damn sure he wasn't going to give him his trust until he earned it.

"You'll change your mind." Angel put up his hand to stop Carr's retort. "Just listen."

Carr nodded, not liking the tone this had taken.

"Early this morning, right after we landed, your siblings and I went for a run in the woods north of Tahoe." Unreleased energy had Angel drumming his fingers on the table.

"You arrived earlier than they told me." Carr wished he could get inside Angel's head.

As if searching for the right words, Angel folded his hands. "We wanted time to explore and understand the territory. We were running through the woods and saw a campfire where there shouldn't have been one." Angel paused, seeming to let Carr digest his words.

Carr's gut tightened, his jaw clenched. "Let me guess, Jokul sent men to find Phaedra and Margo." His words echoed around the room in a low growl.

"He did. It was Brody though, who discovered them. We were going to change our route when something must have caught his attention. Brody said it was a gut instinct or a sixth sense of some sort. He ventured close enough to overhear the conversation. What he heard, he didn't like and he returned for the rest of us."

"It was about Margo and Phaedra." Carr had never felt terror so intense than when danger threatened his wife. He didn't know if he could continue to live if anything happened to her. Wishing he'd been with the group wouldn't make it so.

"Jokul had sent them. He knew Phaedra was in the Tahoe area, and when he could no longer find her, he had his suspicions the girls, Margo and Sophie, were here also. His soldiers were sent to find and bring Phaedra and Margo home. Apparently he didn't care about Sophie."

"But they couldn't find the women, could they?" Momentarily pleased with himself and his newfound ability to cloak, Carr sat back.

"No. We decided we wanted your wedding to go off without a hitch. Brody called us in and we fought them, leaving Jokul's men a clear message. Stay away or all will die. But I don't think the message will deter Jokul from his mission. The man we assumed was the leader was nearly killed before he called his men to evacuate the area."

Carr leaned back in his chair, balancing it on its two back legs while he thought. "The soldiers will report to Jokul but they didn't accomplish their mission." Carr leaned forward. "He won't give up. His men will return, and we'll have to be ready."

"The precautions taken must be well thought out. Jokul's men now have an idea about our strengths and weaknesses. The first encounter was a surprise." Angel rose from the table, looking toward the door of the powder room.

"I believe," Carr rose to stand beside Angel, "we've done all we can for now. It's up to Jokul to make the first move."

"And if the ice demon can't find Margo and Phaedra? What then? They will continue to live with fear."

To end this, he would have to let Jokul hear from Phaedra. He'd have to drop the shield of protection around the two women. His gut cried out to him, saying no, but he knew a confrontation was the only way to be rid of the eminent threat and fear.

"I will have to let down the shield." Revealing Phaedra and Margo to that man wasn't something he wanted to do. Only out of necessity, and for peace of mind for his mate, would he cave in to this action. If he could shield her for the rest of their lives he would, but he knew Margo wanted an end to the life of running, fear and hiding she'd endured for so long.

"Can you do that?" Angel focused on Phaedra who emerged from the ladies room.

"It's the last thing I want." A steal band of fear twisted around his heart, tightening with each breath.

"We will need to meet with your brothers." Angel held out his hand to Phaedra. She accepted and they walked to the table together.

Carr draped an arm across Margo's shoulder and pulled her in for a hug and a quick kiss. He didn't want to be the one to break the news to her. The fear would return, but he agreed with Angel. He wouldn't tell her until the morning.

They ordered another drink and artichoke & spinach dip for a snack. His thoughts revolved around savoring these moments before all hell would break loose. If he didn't tell her, she'd figure it out and her anger was not a valued emotion.

"What would you like to do tomorrow? We could go for a swim, take a picnic lunch." He drew in a deep breath then let it out slow. A few more days then he'd let down the protective shield.

A few more days.

"Is that a good idea?" She fiddled with the ring on her finger.

"The best."

Angel slanted him a fierce look. "You might want to rethink that."

Mind your business, came to mind but Carr turned his attention to Margo. "Let's start with Sophie. After breakfast tomorrow we can see her and play in the backyard. We'll decide then what we should do."

Another drink and with the appetizer almost gone, Angel rose and held out his hand to Phaedra. "Let's go upstairs and leave the newlyweds some privacy."

Watching them leave the bar, Carr wondered why they weren't in their room making love. He wanted Margo, yet he felt the fraud. Not telling her what he and Angel had discussed didn't feel right.

"What's bothering you?"

Margo's question surprised him and drug him from his inner thoughts. "You can tell. Are you part seer too?"

"No, it's the pained expression in your eyes and," she touched his cheek, "No dimples."

"You read me like a book."

Her smile looked wistful to Carr. "I know you and Angel discussed something. You can tell me in our room. And Carr, I really need to get out of the gown. It's beautiful and fits me like a glove but I want to put on my old sweatpants and t-shirt."

"Getting you out of your dress sounds like a plan to me. We could get naked and cuddle." He so wanted to forget what he and Angel had talked about, at least until the sun rose on a new day.

"Not before you tell me what was discussed when I was out of hearing distance." She rose and turned to the elevator. Over her shoulder, "You coming?"

Carr left money for the drinks and appetizer then sprinted to catch up to Margo, darting inside the elevator before the doors closed.

"You were really going to leave without me." He wasn't sure what he thought about that.

"I would have held the doors open." She grinned and pushed the elevator button to take them to the fourth floor.

"Really." He pulled her into his arms and kissed her, feeling the love from head to toe. Their tongues played and danced. She leaned into him then her arms were around him, tugging him closer. He heard her groan as the doors opened on the third floor and a couple stepped inside.

"We're going up," Carr told them, hoping they would wait for a down elevator.

"Us too. Newlyweds?" The question sounded sincere as if they understood the escalating emotions between the couple.

Carr leaned against the wall, but refused to let go of Margo. He held her in front of him, his hands around her waist. When the door opened, he nodded at the intruding couple before he left.

Margo wrapped her arm around his waist and rested her head against his chest as they walked to their room. This was the tranquil moment before the tempest.

He slipped the cardkey inside the lock.

They were inside his suite. "I'm going to change." She disappeared into the bedroom.

Thoughts of following her and making love to her swirled in his head, but he knew better. If anyone should know, she should. He wondered if Angel had spoken to Phaedra yet.

Two bottles of water sat on the coffee table when Margo strode from the room, looking sexy as hell in the snug t-shirt and leggings she wore.

"No sweatpants?" He took the lid off the water and handed it to her.

"Nope." She took a long drink. "Thanks, now, let's get down to business. What's the plan? You and I both understand this one fact. If I'm ever to be free of Jokul, we have to initiate a confrontation. Otherwise Phaedra and I will spend the rest of our lives running and hiding. Don't know about you, but I've spent too much of my life doing just that. So, husband of mine, what are you, Angel and the rest of your clan up to?"

Carr shrugged. "No plan yet. But you understand I'll have to take away the protective cloaking. Sounds good in theory but I don't know if I'll be able to do that."

"You can. We'll have to be ready for him and his men. I think once he finds me, he'll come himself."

Carr shook his head. "I don't think so. He's not going to risk putting himself in danger. The demon's a coward." He pulled Margo into his arms, her back against his chest. He played with her hair, loving the scent and the softness, knowing he never wanted to let her go.

"There's something else you're not telling me." She turned around.

He planted a gentle kiss on her lips. "My siblings, along with Angel had a confrontation in the woods today with some of Jokul's men." He went on to tell her the rest of the story.

"But you defeated them, and easily from what you just said. Why would he risk another loss?"

"Good point. It's my gut telling me. I've no other reason. I believe he will send more men."

"Then your life will be at risk. I don't want that." Her voice shook with emotion. He brushed a tear from her cheek.

"You do care." He smiled. "I'm hoping for love one day."

"I care deeply. Besides, if you don't win, I will find myself on the run. I don't have the crystal, so I can't jump forward in time. It would not take Jokul long to find me." She leaned back against Carr.

"I'm not going to let anything happen to you or Sophie. I promise. But I think you should tell me if her father is in this mix." Carr shut his eyes for a moment. God, but he prayed every second he wasn't giving her false hope.

He watched her sigh and shake her head. "No, her father is dead. He died in a firestorm in Colorado."

"I'm sorry for that."

"Don't be. He betrayed me and Sophie. I don't want to talk about it anymore. It's the past and should stay there."

"All right. I don't want to think of him either." He swept her into his arms and strode to the bedroom. "I want to think of you and sex with you and the love I feel for you." He set her on the bed then came down beside her.

Tracing the line of her jaw, he watched her eyes. The sadness had returned. He had to find a way to replace the sparkle. He kissed her, holding back the raw emotions he felt. They undressed each other, eager for the lovemaking to follow.

She was silver and twilight and softly shimmering curves. A silken shadow lay between her breasts. Velvet softness gathered at their tips, responding to the cool night air flowing from the open window. He held back a of groan of primal need.

Fuck, I could spend my life looking at her.

Yet he didn't ever want to stop gazing at her any more than he could stop needing to touch and savor and rediscover the softness that was Margo.

He lowered his face between her breasts and inhaled a long not-so-steady breath.

The scent brought on thoughts of fire, lace and silk as well as the silver moon glow.

He brushed his cheek against the firm slope of one breast, then the other. When he discovered a silken nipple, he lifted his head. His mouth opened and his breath sighed out around her.

With a mercuric hunger, he drew the nipple into his mouth. Licking, sucking, cherishing, he molded it into a sleek hardness that brushed against his tongue beseeching for more.

If things go wrong for us tomorrow, this might be the last hours we spend together. This was the first time Carr had ever doubted himself. But so much was at stake, another life in jeopardy.

He needed his soul mate to live forever.

Savoring this moment, he tasted the glossy texture of her nipple again, heating the sweet female flesh, molding it with his lips, drawing it ever tighter.

Hunger swept through him like a wildfire, shaking him. Even as he bent his head to her other breast, thoughts of Jokul entered his mind. Yet he forced the danger away and focused on his woman. Sweeter, hotter flesh waited for his touch. He'd tasted it before but now he claimed her as his very own.

In the most primal and elemental ways, he needed to cherish and explore every inch more than he needed to breathe.

Margo made a sleepy, throaty sound before moving beneath Carr, back arching slightly, both giving herself to him and demanding more of his loving.

The motion was sensual, provocative, but she didn't care. All she knew was she was lying beneath a spectacular, hot male while liquid sparks of heat stroked her.

He was powerful and confident. Protecting her with his life, his mission. She ran her hands across his ripped abs. And all that mattered to her was that she was safe within the sensuous embrace of her shapeshifter. For this one moment, she meant to forget the demons stalking her, forget the fear she'd felt for so long. She could forget everything until the sun rose. Pleasure, wild and hot, spread through her body in expanding rings each one hotter and more intense than the next.

Without warning, a scalding pool of liquid heat coursed through her. She arched in primitive reflex, giving herself to the wonder of her shapeshifter's penetrating and caressing heat.

He smoothed his forehead and stubbled cheeks over the top of her thighs. His silky mouth and hard hands followed. The tender raking of his teeth heightened the conflicting textures.

He seduced her legs as completely as he had her breasts. She forgot Jokul still sought her. She forgot the ice and the wind of the ice demon's tower. She forgot everything but the pleasure gathering deep inside her with each kiss he gave her, each caress, each husky word telling her how much he cherished her body.

The stiffness of her legs melted away before his tender assault. Distantly, she realized he was kissing her knees, her thighs, her pussy.

She moaned deep in her throat.

He made a hungry, questioning, oddly soothing sound. Then lifted his head, his dimples showing. "Give me more of this," he said with his low, gravelly voice.

His hands behind her butt, he lifted her and in a fluid motion he was inside her. Fire exploded within and the lazy silver moment vanished. In seconds, she bucked against him crying out his name. "Carr." Her body shuddered and shuddered against him.

"Oh, God Carr."

"Yes, my sweet misbehavin' darlin', yes."

~ * ~

"You're a shifter too?" Phaedra asked.

"Not like the other McKenna's. My alter ego is a wolf. Do you like canines?" He wasn't sure why he asked. He'd felt drawn to her the moment he saw her.

"I don't know."

"You've never had a dog?" He understood Phaedra was a friend of Margo's and he comprehended some of Margo's danger, but he hadn't been told everything.

"No. Jokul the ice demon has kept me prisoner."

Angel's fists tightened, anger simmered down his spine. "Why?" He gritted out, wishing he could chase away her fear.

"I was sent to guide Margo to teach her about her magical abilities and to keep her safe while she grew up. But I showed her how to escape Jokul's ice tower." Phaedra continued with her story.

Angel's grip on reality faded. He didn't want to believe her story but knew it for the truth it was. The need to protect this woman with his life surged through him like a firestorm.

"I won't let anything happen to you. I promise." He meant every word and knew he would die trying.

Her sigh held a hint of laughter. "I know you will try, but don't make promises you might not be able to keep."

"You have little faith." Angel watched her, mesmerized by the way she moved, by the gentle curve of her breasts and the tiny waist he wanted to hold in his hands. She was his opposite in every way.

"You have never met Jokul."

"I have encountered his henchmen and they are harmless fools."

"Jokul is no fool." Inadvertently, Phaedra's hand rose to her neck.

"He has harmed you." Angel watched her tiny gesture and knew it for truth. "Don't deny it."

She let out the breath she'd been holding. "I was his slave. He has hurt me many times and in countless ways. I pray I will never have to see or hear his voice in my head ever again."

"After tomorrow you will have no more fears. Jokul will meet his end tomorrow."

"I hope so. He doesn't deserve to live. Do you have a place to stay tonight?" Phaedra rose from the couch they'd been sitting on. The unlikely couple had spent time discussing the circumstances that had brought both of them to Tahoe.

Angel found Phaedra funny and sincere and now understood her deep fear of the ice demon, Jokul. "I'm not leaving you." He gave the couch a pointed look. "Figured I'd sleep here."

Phaedra bounced on the pillows. "It's pretty hard."

"I've slept in worse places." He shrugged. "Are you handing me an invitation to your bed, pretty lady?"

Amused, Angel watched color stain her cheeks.

"N-no." She stuttered but looked to the room he'd spoken of.

"I'm teasing." They'd held hands most of the night, he'd even kissed the back of her hands but he wouldn't rush her. Wanting her in his bed was a powerful need, but wanting to learn more about her was more powerful.

Chapter Eight

"Eight, nine, and ten, ready or not here I come." Kimi took her hands away from her eyes. "Where are you, Sophie?" Kimi looked under pillows and chairs, under the tablecloth in the dining room. "Where are you?"

She heard a giggle. Lifted the afghan on the couch. "There you are." She bent down and tickled Sophie until tears came to her eyes.

"Now it's your turn."

"Kimi, come look at this." Lyn stood by the window with the curtain pulled back, staring at the front lawn.

Kimi's heart lurched, understanding the tone in her twin's voice. "What is it?"

"Maybe nothing." Lyn turned from the window. "But we might need to take a few more precautions, tighten security so to speak."

"That bad?" Kimi pulled the other half of the curtain back, her breath catching in her throat. "Frost." She whirled to see Sophie playing with her dolls. "At least she doesn't know what is threatening to rip her world apart."

Guy joined them and with a shrug, he spoke. "It's late September. I don't see anything unusual about a small dusting of ice in the mountains. They've probably seen frost here for several days."

"I know, alright, but it could be something else too." Kimi strode to Sophie and sat down, crossing her legs. She picked up a doll and a dress.

"Play with me," Sophie said, holding the doll aloft for a moment before resuming her play.

"You bet." Kimi clothed one of the dolls. Sophie held hers out. Focusing on the frost and the ever-present danger, Kimi dressed Sophie's doll too. She wished she had the ability to see into the future. Shapeshifters didn't have other talents besides shifting.

"I'm going outside to have a look around. Lyn, you call Carr." Brody slipped on his jacket and plopped a cowboy hat on his head.

"I'm coming with you." Guy's jacket lay on the couch. He picked it up and shrugged into it.

After the men left, the room seemed to hold an unexplainable chill. Sunlight filtered through lace curtains and caught the dust motes floating in the air. Sophie sang along with a tune, coming from her LeapPad.

"I'll be right back, honey." Kimi stood and dusting off her hands, she walked back to the window. Lyn hadn't left. She stood as if paralyzed gazing at the yard and the little white picket fence. "Shouldn't it melt?" She looked at the weather app on her cell phone. "It's forty-four degrees outside."

"What do you think? My gut says this isn't from natural causes." Investigating was Kimi's love. She liked to get into the middle of everything and ferret out the evildoer. She'd always found the culprit when she was in school. She remembered the time Jimmy Joe set a garbage can on fire. He would have gotten away with it if she hadn't found the clues leading straight to him.

"Cut the drama," Lyn said. "The guys will be back soon. Let's wait and see what they've got to say."

"Wait and see, I hate those words. And I can tell from the way you haven't left the window, you're worried too." Kimi leaned against the wall, crossing her arms beneath her breasts and watching Sophie. "She's so cute and innocent. I hope she stays that way for a long time."

"I know you hate waiting, but this time we have to abide by the rules of the game, and keep Sophie from harm." Lyn snatched her gaze away from the yard.

"A year ago, for you, it would have been full speed ahead and damn the torpedoes. You were the epitome of impulsive." Kimi wasn't impulsive just inquisitive, their mother had told her too inquisitive for her own good. Her mom had called it by other names such as snooping and prying and even meddlesome.

Lyn shrugged. "My near-death experience changed me, thank you. I'm ready to defend hearth and home, put my life on the line if the need presents itself, but I'm not chasing danger. If Brody tells me to stay here and make sure Sophie stays safe, that's what I'll do."

"I'm sorry." Kimi rested her hand on Lyn's shoulder then gave her a big hug. "I wasn't there. I forgot." She could have lost her twin that day. Thank God, the men had thought to circle back to the ranch. If they hadn't, both Sadie and Lyn would have been lost.

"It changed me in ways I would have never dreamed. I appreciate little things more." She pointed to Sophie contented and playing with her dolls. "The scent of roses, the wind whispering through my hair on a summer day, snowfall. The list goes on until I can't think any longer."

"Do you ever talk about it? That day and what happened."

"My near death? I went to a psychiatrist. But Gramps helped the most."

"The medicine man, of course. I miss him."

"Miss him too. Haven't been to his ranch since the incident with the Amazonian devil." Lyn focused on the yard again. "When I was a little girl, I understood we were different but I never believed for a second there were others out there."

Kimi knew her twin had changed but she'd never understood why. McKenna's were fearless. Perhaps only the men were made up that way. Lyn had seemed so much stronger than her. She'd always thought it was the one factor that made them not quite so identical.

"Want to tell me about it?" Was she being meddlesome or inquisitive? One trait sounded less intrusive than the other.

"I guess. The death experience is so strange. I saw Gramps, chanting and that's what kept me here on earth. Without his healing words, I think my soul would have drifted away. That was all. I didn't float above my body or see into the future or a golden light calling me to heaven."

"Just Gramps. I felt his strength and his courage. He clung to me and pulled me from death's grip. And Carr, I think his presence was with me too."

"In ways, he's the strongest most stable man I know, even more so than Dad. Now I think we need to get Sophie some lunch, and shouldn't Brody and Guy be back?"

Lyn looked out the window again but saw no one. "I don't like this. I think I worry more now than ever. They could text and let us know what they are up to. The only reason I can think of that they wouldn't..."

"They're busy with someone else," Kimi interjected, not liking the direction of her thoughts.

"No, they're men. They don't think of those things. They've never played the waiting game.

"My gut is churning and my heart racing. I don't want a surprise visit. We need a plan." Kimi paced the room, back and forth. "If something has gone wrong, we will have to protect Sophie and at the moment, I feel like the proverbial sitting duck."

Lyn's cell chose that moment to beep. The text said, "Carr and I are eating breakfast. He'll be over soon. I'm going to stay here with Phaedra."

"What is it?" Kimi held out her hand to look at the phone.

Kimi read the message. "It's from Margo. Okay that wasn't the one we were waiting for but it's reassuring."

"It would be just like Brody to try and chase away the demon that is plaguing Carr without involving him." Lyn put the phone in her jeans pocket. Her hands followed and she rocked back on her heels.

The crash in the kitchen sent shock waves of fear through Kimi, her heart lurching to her throat. "What's that?"

"We're here, sorry about that." Brody's large form emerged through the kitchen door, Guy's followed. His cheeks reddened when he saw the girls. "Didn't mean to scare you ladies."

Kimi's hand rested above her heart, "Oh you didn't." Her body shook with the terror the unexpected arrival of the men created.

Brody ruffled her hair. "Little liar," then his tone turned serious. "We have some things to discuss."

Kimi felt the blood drain from her face, to pool in her feet. "Don't like the sound of that. Do we need to sit down?"

Brody roughed his hands through his hair, his expression grim. "Yes."

"Nothing ever changes, you don't mince words." Lyn strode to the couch and sat down.

Kimi felt her knees starting to buckle. She grabbed the windowsill, bending over, she tried to inhale deep breaths. Oxygen didn't want to fill her lungs. The floor spun in crazy circles.

"I got ya." Brody was beside her, sweeping her into his arms and carried her to the couch.

She closed her eyes, letting her big brother take charge. She usually wanted to be independent but the thought of her butt on the hard wood floors of Margo's house would embarrass her.

Guy pulled up a dining room chair, turning it around so he straddled the seat and rested his forearms on the back. "Good job, big bro. Scare them half to death—twice."

Brody shot his little brother a formidable glance but didn't say anything to him.

"Spit it out." Lyn folded her hands on her lap, her back straight and her eyes challenging him as they squinted. "We'd rather understand what we're up against, than not know."

Kimi couldn't talk. Her lips didn't seem to be in working order. At least she could breathe again.

Brody looked to the window then the kitchen as if waiting for all hell to break loose. "We think the frost in not natural. We know..." he amended. "It's too warm for frost, yet it doesn't melt."

Silence stifled the air and Kimi couldn't breathe again. Then it was Jokul. He knew they were in Tahoe and was sending a message.

"Well, it's the ice demon." Lyn fidgeted where she sat. "What do you want us to do?"

Brody put his hands up as if he could stop the thoughts flying through her's and Lyn's minds. "Don't jump to conclusion."

"But you just said..."

"We have no proof." Brody sat down on a chair opposite the girls. "I'm going to pick up Carr and we're going exploring. You all should be fine here."

"And you know this how?" Lyn stood, her face red and her hands fisted at her sides.

Kimi knew her twin. Lyn was about to explode with rage.

"Calm down, Sis. I'm sure Brody will explain." Kimi reached over and tugged at Lyn's hand, hoping she would understand and sit.

"There are some things you might not know about Carr."

"We know he's a goofball and he loves to play around. He lives his role as the second son to the fullest. No strings attached was his motto." Kimi knew Carr better than the rest of the siblings and she understood other things about Carr everyone else overlooked. Carr hid his serious side from everyone in the family except her. He'd once told her there was something wrong with him. He could do things no one in their family could. Once, he'd healed a wolf cub who'd been trapped in a snare. He'd wanted to talk to Gramps about it, but was afraid.

"That's all in the past. It seems he's the leader of all of the McKenna clans around the world." Brody went on to explain the how's and why's and that he had the power to cloak things and keep harm at bay.

Kimi almost told them about his other power but stopped herself. The tale wasn't hers to tell. Carr had sworn her to silence and she'd promised to keep the secret for him.

Once again, silence hung in the room. Lyn broke it. "Okay, so we'll be safe here. I get that."

"The safest place for all three of you will be inside this house."

"Where and when are you going?" Kimi tried for calmness she didn't feel.

"We're going to the woods and we'll shift. We're looking for Jokul's men. I think they are nearby."

~ * ~

Margo touched her lips where Carr had kissed her goodbye. The door shut, and for several seconds she stared at the emptiness. Fear was real and seemed to be ever-present in her life. Wishing it away never worked.

"Margo."

"What, oh..."

"You were lost in thought. I understand, but we need to take this time to practice." Phaedra seemed to watch her with a look that said she'd tolerate no arguments.

"Practice what?" Margo smoothed her shirt with her hands, trying to focus on Phaedra's suggestion.

"Your powers. Fire can be a powerful weapon if used wisely. You need to learn how to direct its path and if something is frozen, you should know how to unfreeze it without causing it harm."

Margo's eyes narrowed, knowing her friend was a seer and she knew things before they happened. "What aren't you telling me?"

"I can see into the future, sometimes. And there have been times I haven't seen correctly. So, we are going to practice until you get it right."

A shiver of panic clawed its way up her spine. Someone she knew and cared about was going to be frozen, and she now had to learn a method to thaw them without killing. "I can't do it."

"You have no choice. If what I've seen comes to pass, someone you love will die without your help. And if you don't learn how to unthaw them, you'll never forgive yourself. Am I right?"

"Yes, but I never bargained for this. What if I can't save them?"

"You need to stay positive."

"You're right."

"Of course I'm right." For a moment, Phaedra's laughter lightened the dreary mood.

"What do I do? So far I've started fires when I was angry and by accident. I've never directed the flames anywhere."

Phaedra set an ashtray on the travertine floor in the bathroom then crumpled up a piece of paper to use as fuel. "Put your hand up so your palm is facing the ashtray."

Margo raised her arm, her fingertips to the ceiling. "Now what?"

"You need to think about fire and focus your energy to that little piece of paper."

Margo nodded, closing her eyes and taking in a deep breath of air, she did as directed.

Nothing happened.

Phaedra crinkled her brow. "I think you have to open your eyes, sweety."

"What? Oh, okay." This time, with her eyes open, the paper smoldered but didn't erupt in flames.

Phaedra clapped her hands together and laughed. "Good job. You're getting the idea."

"Smolder and smoke is not going to stop Jokul." Her sarcasm hit a home run. "I'm going to have to do better."

"Don't be impatient. That was your first try and look what you did." Margo pointed. "Girl, you can start fires. Let's try again." The paper flamed and burned to ashes.

"We have to be careful. I don't want to set the smoke alarms off." Margo looked to the ceiling and the sprinklers. "We could get a thorough drenching if I get too good at this."

"We'll keep the fire little. What you need to do is explore your powers. One tiny piece of paper on flames won't set anything off. Practice makes perfect."

For the next hour, Margo set fire after fire. Each one flamed sooner than the one before it. They opened the bathroom window to let the smoke filter through the opening. Phaedra stood by with a makeshift fan directing the airflow.

"Are you as hungry and tired as I am?" Margo asked.

"Yes." Phaedra picked up the phone to call room service. "It's time for a break. What do you want to have for lunch?"

"Turkey on rye, everything on it."

Phaedra placed the order for two sandwiches. Margo sat on the couch, and leaning back, she closed her eyes. A few moments rest was needed. While she was practicing her newfound skills, she hadn't realized how draining the work had been.

When the knock sounded, both women jumped. Margo's hand flew to her chest as if she could slow her pounding heart.

"Who is it?" Phaedra called out.

"Room service."

Phaedra peeked through the tiny hole on the door. "Okay," she told the waiter and opened it for him to enter.

The man brought the food inside and set it on the table. Phaedra tipped him and he left.

Margo rested her head in her hands, thinking of Carr and praying he wasn't the one who would need unthawing. She was no longer sure she was hungry but the first bite changed her mind.

She was ravenous. When she finished, she said, "I think I can eat two of these."

"Have a chocolate instead." Phaedra opened the sack and brought out a chocolate mint for both of them.

"You are wonderful." Margo popped it in her mouth, savoring the deliciousness.

"I remembered how much you loved those. You can have mine too." She pushed the small candy toward Margo.

"I couldn't."

"Of course you can." Phaedra laughed. "Remember when we were young and had no cares at all?"

Margo nodded, "I always ate yours too. Now back to work."

Margo wiped her lips before setting the napkin on the table. "What do we have to do?"

"Did you forget so soon?"

"Everything has vanished from my head." Margo felt a bit sheepish. "Guess I'm just tired."

Phaedra reached over and took Margo's hands in hers. "I'm sorry but you won't regret this time we're spending. I promise."

Still confused and unable to remember what Phaedra spoke of, she said, "You're going to have to remind me."

"You need to learn how to control your fire to a slow and only warm simmer. The knowledge to unthaw a person is invaluable."

"Right." Margo felt sucker punched. She didn't want to believe one of her friends or Carr would be that person. But Phaedra seemed persistent and she wouldn't be that way if she hadn't seen something.

They worked tirelessly for the next few hours. Timing was everything. Phaedra would set out an ice cube and time how long it took Margo to change the frozen object into a pool of water.

Hours ticked by with little spoken between the two women. The sun set and darkness descended. Stars twinkled in the night sky. Phaedra continued teaching.

"I can't do it!" Margo, frustrated and angry with her lack of ability, threw up her hands.

"Yes, you can." Phaedra's words were slow and determined. "You will not give up. I won't let you."

"Maybe we're going about this all wrong." Margo let out a huge sigh and plopped onto the couch. "Remember the little booklet you gave me when I left the first time?"

Margo nodded.

"I put it together for you, believing the time would eventually come for you to leave. Do you still have it?"

"No, I lost it a long time ago."

"Well, we can't cry over what we can't find." Phaedra sat down, putting her head in her hands. "Give me a moment. I might remember."

Margo listened to her friend's mumbling and posturing. Margo was hit with the urge to laugh. While Phaedra struggled with her memory, Margo ordered pizza. The deliveryman arrived and left.

Margo ate several pieces, watching her friend. "Hungry?"

Phaedra waved her away. "No."

An hour passed, and Phaedra appeared more depressed than ever. Margo wandered into the kitchenette. She dumped out a couple of ice cubes. This time instead of standing away from the frozen lump, she placed her hand a quarter inch away, leaving a tiny space between the ice and her flesh.

Focusing all of her attention on her purpose, she willed the warmth to flow from her hand into the ice. The closeness seemed to work a bit better than the distance. Would she be able to get close to the person she was supposed to thaw?

She tried again and again then one more time. With each new effort, the ice melted slower than the last.

"Phaedra, Phaedra, come see." Margo whirled to see Phaedra watching her from the door. "I did it." Like a schoolgirl, Margo clapped her hands together, excitement pulsing through her.

"Let me see." A huge smile formed on Phaedra's face. "I knew you could do it."

Margo breathed in deep and pulled another cube from the tray. Setting it on the saucer, she let her hand hover above it. This time, she closed her eyes, imagining one of her new friends and praying she could melt the ice so slowly the person would survive.

She didn't want to think of Carr, but she did, knowing with him, she would be the most emotional.

Slow, slow, slow, a small and light stream of warmth, nothing more. Minutes later, when she finished, all energy seemed to have drained from her. She sat down, closing her eyes and letting her head fall on the back of the couch.

"You're exhausted from that small effort." Phaedra sat beside Margo. "Rest."

"I can't imagine how I would feel if I had to do that to a person. It's so much easier to toss fire. Anger is a powerful tool but so is determination. I've got to remember the incredible amount of control I need for this."

"You do." Phaedra swiped pizza from the table. She watched Margo. "You're ready for anything Jokul tosses your way."

"I wish I had your confidence." Not only was she exhausted but her stomach was rolling and every muscle in her body ached.

Her gaze focused once more on Margo. "You're going to need a healer when this is done."

Margo laughed outright. "Where do we pick one of those up? Not like we're going to find one in the corner store."

"Honestly, I don't know." Phaedra played with the pepperoni on her slice. "I don't know. Perhaps my misgivings are for naught. Maybe time will restore you."

"Well, we don't know what will happen. I'm tired of second guessing everything."

"You are right. We should let the events unfold."

"Shouldn't Carr and Angel be back?"

~ * ~

Jokul paced the turret of his ice castle, pumping his fist. He was close, so damn close he could smell victory. Atantsi and Phaedra were in Tahoe. He knew it. All he had to do was find her. She was going to have to come out of hiding some time.

And when she did...

"Come here." Jokul motioned for his new slave to enter the room. She carried a tray of food and drink. "Put it there." He pointed to the table inside. "I'll be there in a moment."

She nodded and did as he said.

From sheer joyous malice he tightened the girl's collar, delighted to hear her gasp in surprise. He watched her finger try to slip under the collar in a futile attempt to loosen it. And he loved her thoughts. *She'd kill me if she could.*

He let out a bellow of laughter. Fuck, he couldn't remember her name but he knew where he'd found her, and she'd never go back. The amber alert had gone off but it was too late. Once more, laughter filled his heart and soul.

She'd been a virgin the first time he'd fucked her. When he got Phaedra back, he'd let the girl watch them and he'd make Phaedra teach the child-woman. Laughter bellowed from him again.

Stepping inside, he tasted the fried mozzarella and poured a glass of wine. The girl cowered in a corner of the room, her mind no longer sizzling with hate. He cocked his head, staring at her then motioned for her to come to him.

"Try the food." She looked at him with fear-filled eyes. "Go ahead. I won't hurt you if you do as I say." He stroked her flesh at the line of her dress then across her collarbone. She flinched, but when he tightened the collar again, she froze.

He handed her a strawberry.

"Thank you."

"Sit by me," he told her and pulled her beside him on a couch. "Would you like wine?"

She didn't know what to say. He'd reprimanded her once when she accepted and once when she'd said no. *Good*, keeping her wondering was intriguing.

"Go ahead." Jokul urged her.

She accepted the glass and sipped. He smiled but did nothing, enjoying her confusion.

"Sir?"

The interruption angered him. "What do you want?"

"We have news of the shapeshifters."

Chapter Nine

Carr picked up Angel at Phaedra's door then the pair met Brody and Guy in the forest north of Tahoe. Leaves on the Aspens shimmered where sunlight danced and played. A soft breeze filled the air with the scent of pine needles. Yet everything about the scene was wrong.

"Look at that." Carr, along with Angel, stepped from the vehicle, motioning with his hand, sweeping in a three hundred sixty degree circle. "It's frosted, all of it, the land, the trees and shrubs. This is Jokul's signature."

"I would not believe it if I wasn't seeing it with my eyes." Angel tipped his hat back, staring at the scene. "I've been around the world several times and visited every continent. If I didn't know what it was, I'd say this is one of the most beautiful sights I've ever seen."

Brody and Guy stepped from their car, walking to meet Angel and Carr. "My gut is talking to me and it's not telling me anything I want to hear."

"Do we have a plan?" Brody asked.

Looking over the lake, ripples caught shafts of sunlight. The forested hills on the opposite side appeared an iced-over dark blue. Frogs croaked and birds sang in the trees above. A squirrel dashed up a pine tree.

"So normal and yet..." Carr closed his eyes and listened to the forest. "There is trouble a foot. The animal's chatter tells us of an ice castle in the mountains. And a raging demon."

Carr shielded his eyes to study the rocky-topped mountains before turning to his brother. "I'm supposed to have powers other than shifting. Not sure what they are." That wasn't quite true. He suspected the power of healing was his. He'd just never thought to use it. God, if he'd known, he could have healed Lyn when the Amazonian Devil almost killed her. Did he have other powers too?

"But you suspect something?" Brody was relentless when it came to telling the truth. "Before we embark on this journey, we should know and understand your magic."

"I agree, but Gramps said I would discover them when they became necessary for survival. I suspected a long time ago I could heal. But when Lyn was hurt, I didn't even think of trying and I can't figure out why. He said it was instinctual. Wouldn't a life and death situation bring out my healing power?"

"So you have your doubts," Brody said. "Didn't you sit by her through her recovery? Did you hold her hand, or speak to her? Perhaps you did heal Lyn."

Carr nodded. "I can't say. There is no verification. I need proof." He paused, fists clenching for several long seconds. "If we run into Jokul or his men, I wish I knew what I could do. My powers, are they good? I mean will they work if I'm in my cat form? I don't like going into this with so much on the line and not understanding myself or my abilities or even knowing..." He shrugged, feeling as confused as hell. His gut still churned and his nerves were stretched so thin he thought they might snap.

"What you cannot do seems more important." Angel chimed into the conversation.

"Thanks, pal." Carr wiped sweat from his forehead, staring at the lake and thinking a good cooling off would be nice. "It's fuckin' hot for all this ice to be coatin' the ground."

"We should shift and explore this side of the forest around the east side to the north. We could head into the mountains. I'm sure Jokul likes it best where it's the coldest. He could be perched on some mountaintop." Brody pointed northward. "Let's get these clothes off and see what's on the other side."

Carr packed a change of clothes for each of them. The backpack, he slung over his shoulders before he shifted. The sensations began at his toes, and adrenalin surged through him. He closed his eyes, allowing the powerful forces to complete their task.

When he opened his eyes, he was on all fours, his tail twitching and ready. A quick look around showed him the others had completed their transformations as well. He smiled when he saw the huge wolf that was Angel. They would work well together.

Brody took the lead, and Carr trailed after them to guard the rear. It was the way they had always proceeded. His protective nature coming into play, he liked his place in the back of the pack.

As they padded along, Carr's thoughts turned toward the possibility of ambush. The trail was narrow and it would be easy for Jokul's men to hide in the trees or in the dense shrubbery.

An ambush is a quite reasonable thought. This came from Brody.

Carr wasn't sure if the others heard. He'd always had the ability to read his sibling's mind when in cat form. Was this another power? One he should try to develop? Hell of a time to be distracted.

Yes, I hear you too. Angel spoke to him. *But I can't hear Brody or Guy's thoughts.*

He telegraphed to the others that he could hear their thoughts. The communication would serve them well when they found Jokul. His body surged with unleashed energy.

So much for privacy when he could hear all of the others.

They paced themselves, following a narrow trail, winding ever higher. Carr wasn't sure why Brody set their path on this course. However, it was in this general direction they had found Jokul's men who had been setting up camp for the night. But he didn't think they were stupid, didn't believe they would find the men in the same place. But Brody sensed things others did not and he was rarely wrong.

Brody, do you have a destination in mind? Carr sent his thought to his brother and waited for an answer.

I do. I'm looking for Snowflower Mountain. I heard something unusual was sighted on the rocky ledge. A helicopter pilot said it was the most extraordinary sight, almost reminded him of an ice castle."

"Fuck, I didn't expect that." Carr sniffed the air, catching no unnatural scents on the breeze.

After a few hours, they stopped to rest, each standing guard while the other could eat and sleep. They traveled best at night. Brody figured it would take another day to reach the mountain. His restless energy had him pacing the campsite. He needed a good fight.

~ * ~

The sun began its descent in the western sky, sending a fiery glow across the lake and mountains. Carr rose and stretched, purring to himself as the kinks in his muscles worked themselves free of the tightness. Even though the night had seemed never-ending, he felt refreshed and energized.

As they started to climb the rocky trail, the sky darkened and the wind began with a slow hum reaching a thundering crescendo in a matter of seconds. Without warning, Carr found himself sucked into a whirling vortex. He spun through the dark tunnel, tumbling and turning, bouncing off imaginary walls until he felt bruised from head to toe. Yet the churning continued until his lungs were dry and his body exhausted.

He watched the others as they all seemed to spin through the whirlwind with him. His stomach churned even as his cat senses programmed him to land on his feet. A pin of light filtered through the darkness of the tunnel. Carr kept his focus on the shimmering light. Still, the four shifters tumbled through the twisting cyclone.

He fell into Brody then Angel. Curses echoed through his head. Not only were they bouncing off the barriers that held them prisoner, but each other as well.

Streaks of light sparkled through the tunnel, flashing off black walls. The pinhole crept closer. Carr realized he needed to fine-tune all his senses. His heart raced with anticipation and his nerves zapped energy through his body. Jokul was making the steep climb to his ice tower much easier and faster.

After what seemed like hours, Carr slid onto a slippery cold surface, Brody hitting his back as he came to a halt. The others plowed into the one in front. The world in front of him spun. He shook his head in an attempt to slow the world's movement.

Loud screams pierced the silence. Guns in hand, men jumped from above, forming a circle around the four shifters. Dazed and reeling from their unnatural flight, Carr could not react. They were surrounded and captured without a fight. His heart pounded and he searched for someway to defeat Jokul and his men.

A man's laughter penetrated the icy cliff and Carr's mind. "So you have come to end the great Jokul." The ice demon stepped through the circle of men. His hands behind his back, he walked toward Carr. "Do I kill you all in your shifter form or have you change back? Hmmm...so many decisions."

Carr felt the evil and fought the urge to rip Jokul's heart from his chest. He heard his brother speaking to him. *Calm yourself and think.* It wasn't the first time he'd listened to his brother's advice and he prayed it wouldn't be the last.

Well that was a good idea but all this had happened so fast, they weren't prepared. Going down without a fight had not been his plan. He let out a loud roar, shaking the ice columns and sending a vase to clatter on the floor.

Don't give up. Jokul has not defeated us and he won't. You must remain composed and in control. We are more powerful than the ice demon.

Surrounded as they were, words from Brody seemed futile and useless. To react now would mean death to all. If he did not survive this, he prayed Margo and Phaedra would find a way to end Jokul.

Jokul walked around the shifters. "Which one of you is the favorite of Margo? I wonder." He stopped by Brody. "The pure black one or this golden cat?" He started to put one finger under Brody's chin and was met with snapping teeth. "Is it you?"

Cloak your mind against him, Brody cautioned.

The warning came too late.

"Ah." He turned to Carr. "I can feel the hate and I can hear your thoughts. Did you know hate gives me more strength? No, I don't suppose you do."

Jokul stepped close to the wolf. Angel growled low and threatening. "This one is certainly different, a wolf among cats. Well, the bunch of you can shift back or stay as you are. Makes no difference to me."

Turning to his men, he waved one arm. "Take them to their cells. I'll decide what to do with them later."

"Leave this one here. On second thought, leave them all. I've decided their fate. They will make intriguing ice statues for my new home." Jokul stretched out his arms, pointing his hands at the shifters. Ice streamed toward them.

Slowly, they were covered with frost, a frost turning into ice until Guy, Angel and Brody were frozen statues. Rage bellowed in Carr's head. Emotionally torn, he didn't know where to direct his attention, toward his friend and siblings or Margo and Phaedra. His gut churned with fear and apprehension. No...

Focus on the women, keep them safe and try to warm the ice around you. Carr tried, but as soon as one layer melted away, Jokul shot another icy blast toward him. His strength slipped away, his mind wavering. Dizziness overwhelmed him, his head spinning in frozen circles. Pulling emotions from deep within, he felt ice chip away, his body warming.

The feat was nothing he'd done before. No, something had caused a shift in Jokul's focus. The ice demon no longer concentrated on him. Jokul turned to the south, his brows furrowed together.

Fuck! To Carr this meant one thing. He'd failed to keep Margo and Phaedra cloaked. Had the demon found little Sophie and the twins too? With a fierce resolve, he fought the ice surrounding his body and threatening to penetrate his soul.

The grin spreading across Jokul's face told Carr all he needed. How much time before Margo and Phaedra were captured and brought to this iced over hellhole? He couldn't let that happen.

With more strength and determination, he fought through the layers of ice coating his body. Felt chards of ice rip from his fur, shaking from his tail to his nose, the icicles clattered across the floor. His body rocked with the staggering effort.

At the noise, Jokul turned to him, his hand rose to send more ice Carr's way, but Carr leapt from the spot Jokul had directed the torrent.

Ice coated ice. Again the demon sent a stream of ice his way and once more Carr avoided contact. It was a game of cat and mouse. Carr could not get close enough to stop Jokul, and Jokul's reactions were not as fast as Carr.

The demon's face turned red and ice thundered around Carr. It seemed the castle quaked and trembled with the contact the torpedoes of frozen water made when they hit the floor.

Staying in his cat form for now, Carr understood he was quicker and stronger. Jokul seemed to tire for a moment. Carr leapt toward him but was pushed back with a gut wrenching force. An icy blast knocked the wind from his lungs. He gasped for air and nothing seemed to enter. An inner calm swept through him and he inhaled a long and slow breath of oxygen, then another.

But this gave Jokul time to regain his strength. Jokul spoke to his men. "Do not shoot. This one is mine."

The battle could go on forever, yet at the same time he needed to focus energy and warming powers on his brothers and cousin.

You cannot win this, McKenna.

Jokul's thoughts knifed through Carr's mind as they moved cautiously around each other, each searching for a moment's weakness.

And you think you can?

Jokul laughed. *I have only one focus. You have five if I'm counting right. Do you think you can protect them forever?*

Yes.

You are a bigger fool than I thought, Carr McKenna. Jokul sent a bolt of ice straight toward his heart.

Carr leapt away.

The thunder of ice around him gave Carr new hope. Jokul was weakening. It was just a matter of time. Carr concentrated on freeing Brody first and watched ice slowly melt from Brody's still form.

Suddenly, Brody was in Carr's head. *Don't give up on any of us. You're big brother isn't frozen yet. Heal me and I'll be free to help you.*

Carr smiled inwardly while he watched Jokul. The pair still circled, each trying to gain the upper hand. Jokul threw a powerful strike. Carr jumped at the last second, his heart beating a rapid staccato beneath his chest. For the first time, he believed they might have a chance.

Silence surrounded them, and Jokul seemed to have nothing to say to Carr. Something had changed. Jokul seemed delighted. Carr tried to get inside the demon's mind but to no avail.

Margo...

He heard the demons laughter and knew the women had been found.

~ * ~

Phaedra jerked to immediate defense mode when she heard Jokul's voice inside her head. She focused on the good and beautiful of this world, seeing butterflies and flowers, the scent of roses, in hopes she could block his words.

"What is it?" Margo looked up from the magazine she'd been reading. Setting it on the table, she waited for an answer.

"I hear Jokul." Phaedra hands were clenched together in what appeared a death grip.

"Whatever you do, don't let him know where we are." Margo didn't know if that was possible but she prayed it was. Since Phaedra arrived in Tahoe, she'd learned so much. "Think of somewhere else, lead him in the wrong direction. You can do it." Margo swallowed hard, terror settling in her gut.

"I'm thinking of our country on top the high cliffs of Greece, Angizei ton Ourano and picturing the rugged terrain."

"Good I can see it too. And my parents, they are standing on the turret of our home with open arms to welcome me, the wind whistling around them. I'm walking the steps to the main building."

Phaedra laughed. "It was windy wasn't it? I'd love to go home and feel the sweet caress of the breeze."

"Keep thinking of our homeland. I'm going to gather some things before we leave. If his voice is in your head, it means Carr is in trouble. We have to find them and give aid any way we can." Margo drew in a deep breath. Her insides shook and the dizziness welling around her stemmed from distress. She had to shake lose the terror and fight. She and Phaedra had worked hard. Her skills were no longer questionable but deadly. She could take a life and could bring one back. From the moment Phaedra had told her she needed to learn how to melt ice, keeping a frozen statue alive, she'd known it would come to this.

"Are you ready?" Phaedra stood, her hands clasped together, a solemn expression on her face. "I need to retrieve the crystal from my room first then we will learn what needs to be done."

"I'll go with you and together we will end the ice demon." She wanted so much to check on Sophie but knew that action might bring harm to her little girl as well as the twins.

In a sign of unity, they linked arms and strode to Phaedra's room. She picked up the crystal, and walking onto the balcony, Phaedra held the clear orb toward the sun. "Take us to Jokul, wherever he might be." Phaedra began to chant as the crystal seemed to take on a life of its own.

Splinters of sunlight hit the glass ball. The glow surrounding the crystal flowed into and around the girls. The world turned and spun. All the colors of the rainbow wrapped them in a protective tunnel.

Margo closed her eyes against the blinding light, clinging to Phaedra as they hurtled through space. She felt the difference. Time was not changing, only their destination.

In a matter of seconds, they were set down on a ledge of ice. Laughter echoed through the hallway then thunderous booms. Margo motioned to Phaedra to follow her. With caution, they walked toward the sounds. The building they were in shook and the ice columns around them swayed as if they might fall.

"What is it?" Margo felt nausea roll in her stomach. For a moment, she closed her eyes, hoping to understand what was happening and how to deal with it. She tried to remain composed, knowing the ability to think and react in a rational manner would serve her well.

A young girl cowered in a corner, a collar around her neck. Tears flowed down her cheeks. She turned from them when she saw them, her body trembling.

Phaedra knelt beside her. "Are you Jokul's slave?"

The girl looked up, terror clearly written in her eyes and nodded, "yes."

"Where are they? Where is Jokul? And what is he doing?" Margo's impatience grew exponentially. Fear spiraled, yet she forced control of her emotions and tried to remember everything she'd learned.

"Down that hall. He has killed. The big cats didn't have a chance. He is keeping one alive just to torment him." The girl's shaking hand rose from her lap and pointed.

"You'll be fine." Phaedra cupped the girl's cheek with her hand. "I promise. When this is finished, I will come back for you."

The girl didn't say anything. Instead she stared back with a vacant and torn gaze as if she didn't believe Phaedra.

"Jokul will not survive this day. I promise you. You will be set free." At her sides, Margo clenched and unclenched her fists. She meant to do this and suddenly she was no longer terrified of Jokul, his ice or his threats. With each passing second, her courage and confidence grew.

Several heartbeats later, Margo stepped inside the room where the slave girl sent her. The sight caught her breath. Carr's siblings and cousin were frozen ice statues. Relief that Carr wasn't frozen swept through her. Yet fear for him immobilized her for a moment. She watched him leap into the air, avoiding an ice bolt Jokul shot at him.

So consumed with their fight, neither male noticed their entrance to the room. Time was apparently on her side. Before anyone knew she was there, she shot fire at the three guards, their bodies aflame. The inferno lit the room. Then she turned her attention to the demon. Focusing on Jokul's back, she raised her hand, sending fire his way. Seeming to feel the searing heat, he whirled.

Rage lit his face then a smile. "You have come back to me but it is too late." He sent a torpedo of ice her way. Unflinching, she met it with fire. For a second, confusion creased his brows. She saw determination and rage in his face and a moment of confusion.

"You cannot defeat me." More powerful than ever, he sent another wave of ice towards her.

She met ice with fire. "No, Jokul, I'm not an innocent young girl who has no idea how to use her powers. Phaedra has taught me well. Did you think I would always be weak and in your control?"

Rivulets of water from the melting ice ran across the floor. Carr let out a mighty roar and leapt toward Jokul, bringing him down. They rolled on the floor, Jokul caught between Carr's claws.

At the close proximity, Jokul was able to slather Carr in a coat of frost. He broke free, scrambling to his feet and sending a small coating of frost to entomb Carr.

Margo could not risk Carr's life. Yet she remained ready for the battle, waiting for the right moment. Jokul left his mark on Carr once more. Then he rose, his frown growing.

"I will end you, Jokul," Margo said. "There is no other way." Her arms extended, her hands pointing to Jokul, she was poised on the brink of no return. She recalled the spoken words of caution. If she ended his life, there would be repercussions felt around the world. But if she did not, her life as well as the McKenna's would be threatened.

"You're very certain." Jokul's laughter encased her soul and terrified her. Once again, he sent a stream of ice, and once more she melted it with her fire. "You're no longer the weak little girl who fled my care."

"I told you it was so. I am strong, stronger than you because I have love for these people. You have only hatred to guide you." Her heartbeat slowed and assertive energy surged through her.

Phaedra remained behind Margo. "You must finish this. His strength is great. You must strike now before he regains his energy field. You cannot outlast him and you have the others to think of."

Margo tipped her head slightly, noticing how Carr had thrown off the cloak of frost and was stretching his muscles. While she kept her focus on Jokul, Carr looked at her and nodded.

She heard Carr's words in her mind. *You have no choice. He means to kill all of us if he survives.*

Before Jokul attacked again, she sent streams of fire his way. An inferno engulfed him. His body smoldered from within creating a red glow around his core. The color grew and his body began to melt. Yet Margo continued the flow of fire directed at the ice demon.

Suddenly, Jokul shattered into thousands of tiny particles all sizzling with fire. The castle began to shake and rocks slid from the cliffs above.

The earth shook with a force that sent her to the floor. "Carr!" she cried out his name, and he stood beside her quickly shifting into his human form.

With Margo beside him, he rushed to Brody to begin the healing. Reverently, he passed his hand across Brody's body. Margo didn't take time to watch, she bent beside Angel and holding her hand on his head, she willed the slow warming of his shifter form.

The castle continued to shake even after the quake had finished moving the earth. Rocks and ice fell to the floor around them.

"We must hurry and get off this mountain." Carr's voice penetrated her thoughts.

"If I go too fast, Angel will burn. I must do this right. Go, take the others."

Carr pushed her away. "I will finish. Brody, Guy, get dressed and take the women down the mountain. There is a girl down the hall, Jokul's slave, find her. I will follow with Angel as soon as we can."

"I won't leave you. I'll help. With two of us working on him, he will heal sooner." Margo stood her ground. As long as Carr stayed in this shattered mountain ice castle, so would she.

With wide eyes, she watched as the ice slowly melted from Angel. The moment heat filled his heart and soul she knew, yet the rocks of ice still fell around them as the castle collapsed.

Angel stretched, shaking off the last vestiges of ice, he stood tall and looked proud. Seconds later, he shifted and Carr handed him clothes and took his own jeans from the bag, quickly slipping into them.

Together they scrambled down ledges and dodged falling debris. Margo caught her heel on a rock, yet managed to pull free before Carr stopped to help. She'd give anything for Phaedra's crystal right now, but they were safe and there was nothing she'd change. Choices had been made.

Carr pulled up, stopping them on a precipice. There was nowhere to go except back. He pulled Margo into his arms. The warmth from his embrace gave her courage. "We're going to die here, aren't we?"

"No, we are not. I swear we will find a way down this mountain."

"I wish Phaedra were here with her crystal."

As if Phaedra had heard her wish, they turned and in front of them a brilliant light glowed. Margo put her hand to her eyes to provide a shield for the orb's brilliance.

Her breath caught as it floated closer, seemingly moving in slow motion. After what seemed like hours, the orb stopped and the light formed a figure.

"Phaedra."

"Did you think I'd leave you all to make your way down the mountain side alone?" She sounded indignant. "Of course I would return."

Silence, only silence, Margo was left speechless.

"Come, we have seconds until this ledge disappears. Come." She motioned with her arms and the trio walked to her and formed a circle linking arms.

Phaedra held the orb toward the sun and once more the crystal worked its magic.

Chapter Ten

"Momma." Sophie ran into Margo's open arms. She lifted her, holding on as if she never wanted to let her go. Margo twirled her around and around until she was breathless.

They were in Sophie's and Margo's home, Guy and Brody stood in the background. Kimi and Lyn besides them. Silence stretched between the little group and it seemed no one knew what to say. Sophie shouldn't hear what really happened, but Margo knew Kimi and Lyn were impatient to learn the details.

"We were so worried about you, Sophie. Phaedra volunteered to get you. She was the only one who could. But we chose not to involve anyone in the house," Carr said.

Margo breathed in deeply, studying the faces she saw around her. "What now? Is Jokul gone forever or will he return?"

Carr wrapped his arm around Margo's shoulder, pulling her close and giving her a quick kiss on her cheek. "I believe he is but one can never be too sure about the ice demon."

Guy stepped forward, the youngest of the group, he seemed to have put this latest adventure behind him. "I'm famished. Anyone care if I order pizza and drinks?"

Lyn punched him in the arm. "Ye of little reverence, little bro. Order it up. I'm hungry too. I want to know everything that happened but it can be put on hold so you can feed your bottomless belly. I'm just happy everyone made it back. Waiting is too hard but I really didn't want to be part of the group either."

"A celebration is in order." Kimi seemed to disregard her twin and looked at Sophie. "What kind of pizza do you want? My favorite is the vegie variety but everyone tells me I should love the ones with all the meat on them."

"Pepperoni." She ducked her head into her mother's shoulder. Margo cuddled for a moment, and Carr wrapped his arms around both mother and child.

"Ah, Sophie, you don't need to be shy with me. We played all afternoon. And two hours of hide-and-go-seek should make me a friend. Did you have fun? Or was I imagining things?" Kimi tickled the little girl who snuggled even closer to her mother.

Sophie nodded. "I don't know."

Kimi blinked as if suddenly confused. "What is that supposed to mean?"

"It's her answer for most everything," Margo said, laughing. "I don't know and what the heck. The words usually have no rhyme or reason to them."

"But it is cute," Lyn said.

"Good, I think that's a yes then. You did have a good time. Now for the order." Kimi wrote down all of the favorites then handed the list to Guy with the command. "Don't mess up."

Guy's eyebrow rose a fraction but he didn't comment. A few minutes later, Guy and Lyn left, and the rest of the group settled down to talk. Margo watched the easy camaraderie among the clan. Phaedra stayed close to Angel just as Margo didn't want to move from Carr's side. She didn't want this feeling of euphoria to vanish.

"Tell us everything that happened," Kimi said, sitting down on a chair and leaning forward as if in anticipation.

"We should wait until after we all eat and I can put Sophie to bed." Margo pulled her little girl close, praying nothing like this would ever happen again. "What did you do while we were gone beside play hide and seek?"

Sophie smiled. "I like Kimi. She's really nice. I let her play with me and she shared my toys just like you tell me to do. I didn't go to school though. Will I get in trouble?"

"Of course not. I'll write you an excuse on Monday and get your homework if you have any. Okay?" Margo ruffled Sophie's hair then bent close to her ear. "I love you so much, sweetheart."

They chatted about nonsensical things until Guy and Lyn returned with pizza and beers.

Margo fixed a plate for Sophie then herself. Carr spent time talking with Brody. She wondered what they would all do now. She didn't want to leave her tiny home in Tahoe. Sure Carr would want to return to Cactus Junction, she had decisions to make.

They ate and celebrated with cheers and toasts. Margo watched Sophie cover her mouth to yawn. "I'm going to put Sophie to bed." She held her hand out and Sophie took it.

"I'm not tired," Sophie told her.

Margo laughed, feeling as if her life had become normal for the first time she could remember. "Then why are you yawning?"

Her little hand felt good, and the knowledge Sophie was safe brought new tears to Margo's eyes. The fears from her past seemed far away.

"Will you read me a story?"

"Of course, honey."

"I can do that if you like?" Nanny stood, she'd found a place in the kitchen to eat.

"Thank you so much, but it's been so long since I've been here to read her a story, I'd like to do it."

Margo found clean pajamas then she watched Sophie brush her teeth and helped her wash her face. Her little cheeks had pizza sauce all over them.

When they were finished, Margo said, "Let's pick out a book. Okay."

"I want you to read that one." Sophie pointed.

"It's an Angelina Ballerina story. I like those too." Margo sat down on the bed and patted a spot beside her. Sophie snuggled in close. When the story was finished, Margo pulled back the covers and tucked Sophie into bed. She kissed her on the forehead.

"I love you, Momma." Sophie held out her arms for a hug. Margo bent over and wrapped her arms around the little girl.

"I love you more." Margo left, closing the door behind her. "Sleep tight." For a moment, Margo leaned against the door and closed her eyes. She tried to shut out the horror of the day and remember this time with Sophie.

She walked down the hall and stood outside the living room, surveying the scene. Everyone talked and teased. Angel looked a bit out of place but with Phaedra beside him he seemed more at ease than the last time they were in a room together. Hesitant to step into the room, she watched a bit longer.

Carr saw her. "Margo, good you are finished. We've a lot to talk about." He was sitting in a chair and rose to let her have his place.

She wasn't sure if she did want to sit and she wasn't sure she wanted the story recounted. The terror of seeing her new family frozen still occupied the forefront of her mind. "What have you guys told Lyn and Kimi?"

"Just about everything." Carr motioned for her to sit beside him.

"Yeah, we filled them in and they've decided adventures are overrated," Brody said.

Kimi punched him in the arm.

"Am I wrong?" Brody sounded incredulous, his eyes wide in question. "Or do you just get off hitting me?"

"You're not wrong," Kimi said, leaning back and closing her eyes. "I don't know about the rest of you but I'm just about ready for bed."

"It's late and we've had an exhausting day. But I've questions for all of you." Margo loved the warmth of her hand in Carr's.

"Shoot." Carr ruffled her hair.

"For starters, what are we all doing tonight?" Margo didn't want to spend time away from Sophie and she didn't have enough room in her little place for all of the McKenna clan to stay. She supposed they could settle on the couch and the floor but she needed privacy, some time with Carr, time when her life wasn't threatened.

The McKenna's looked at each other then shrugged. If she wasn't worried about where they were going to sleep, she would have laughed. It seemed in this instance not one of them could make a decision.

"I guess that's up to you and Carr." Brody picked up his hat, examining it with obvious concentration. "I'm betting the newlyweds would like to be alone. And I'm also guessing Margo here doesn't want to leave Sophie. Am I right?" He set his hat on his head, preparing to leave.

"Angel is going to stay in my room in the hotel." Phaedra tugged on Angel's hand. "We should get out of here."

"Good idea." Angel rose and started for the door.

"Wait, we can all go in the car, as soon as we decide where our heads will land." Brody picked up the car keys. "But I also think we need to decide what we're doing tomorrow. My vote is to go home. I'm missing the pleasure of my sweet sexy Sadie."

"You going to fly or drive?" Lyn asked. "I'd like a road trip. Maybe I could take the car and do some exploring on my own. I haven't been to Vegas in a long time. Maybe there's a good show."

"I'll go with you," Kimi said. "To keep you from doing something stupid."

"It's a deal. What about you, Guy?"

"I'd like to fly home with Brody."

"That leaves Angel and Phaedra."

Angel flushed and cleared his throat.

"Well..." Brody persisted.

"I've work to do. I'm going my own way. But if any of you nosy McKenna's are interested, I plan on seeing Phaedra again. I just can't stay right now."

"If it's all right with Margo, I'd like to stay here in Tahoe. I'm not sure what I'm going to do, but perhaps I can find work. The hotel room was paid for two months so I have time."

"You're welcome to come home with us to Cactus Junction. Nanny too." Carr volunteered the information Margo had wondered about. He did expect her to go home with him. Part of her liked the idea and the other part resented his plan, because he'd forgotten to ask her. But she kept silent. This was a topic they needed to talk about in private.

Margo turned to the woman who'd helped her so much. "Nanny, if I decide to go, would you come with us?"

Nanny's smile was huge, her hands clasped at her chest. "I'd love that more than anything."

"Thanks, I'll keep that in mind." Phaedra tugged on Angel's hand, moving toward the door where Brody waited for the family to make up their minds.

"I'll get the girls a room at the hotel. I'll stay with Guy in Carr's room. We'll bring your things over tomorrow if you don't want to come get them. I'm going to file an early flight plan so we'll be taking off around six AM."

"Bring my things here. I'll give you a key and you can set them inside." Carr kissed Margo on the back of her neck.

She grinned, leaning into him. He wrapped his arms around her waist. Margo wiggled free so she could give everyone a hug. "Don't know when I'll see all of you again. Thank you so much for coming to our rescue. I don't know what I, what we, could have done without you." Tears formed and threatened to fall.

"It seems you did all of the saving." Brody laughed. "We'd be ice statues in Jokul's ice palace if it weren't for you and Carr."

"Yeah, I hear you, but Margo and Phaedra would still be running from Jokul. So we needed each and every one of you guys. Thanks," Carr said.

Once again, Carr wrapped his big arms around her, pulling her against his chest so they could watch his clan leave.

As the car Brody rented disappeared from view, Margo turned in Carr's arms. "What do you want to do now?"

"Do you really have to ask that question?"

"No." Margo wanted him and needed physical contact to help chase the demons lingering in her head—vanquished came to mind.

But first, I've something I'd like to give you. One minute." He left the room and returned with a large wrapped package. "This is for you."

"What is it?" Overwhelmed with love for this beautiful man, she wanted to touch him and be with him forever. Her fingers swept over the brown paper wrapping the present.

"Open it and see?"

Excited, she ripped through the wrapping in record pace. Then, struck by the beauty of the gift, she said, "My portrait." Her breath stilled for a second, as did her heart.

"Do you like it?" His quiet voice sounded hesitant.

She laughed. "I love this picture, but I don't know where to hang it. When did you finish it, it's..."

"In our bedroom, baby. Where only I can see it. And I had some alone time. I worked on it then."

He lowered his head and kissed her, their tongues, met and dueled. She leaned into him, heat rushed through her as she melted into his body.

He lifted his head and said in a raspy voice, "I want you to give me more of this." Then he kissed her again, sweeping her into his arms, he settled on the couch with Margo on his lap. "I want to make love to you all night long."

Margo ran her hands through his hair, pulling him downward, needing the feel of his mouth melding with hers.

His hands roamed her body, exploring, touching, exciting every inch. She heard his groan then her own.

"We can't do this on the couch. Sophie..." She turned her head to the side to give him better access to her neck. He kissed and nibbled, his teeth grazing her flesh until he reached her ear. His tongue traced the shell. Her body jerked and throbbed.

"I'm going to have to get used to having a six year old close by, aren't I?" His lips kissed their way across her collarbone.

She shivered and felt the rise of heat. "Yes." She reached beneath his shirt and touched his skin, flesh against flesh. She needed to feel all of him to become one with him. His belt buckle was in easy reach, she undid it, then the button and on to the zipper.

"Just a minute," he whispered next to her ear before pushing away from her. "Hold that thought. I want to get something.

~ * ~

He walked into the bedroom and found candy handcuffs he'd bought the other day. At the doorway, he dangled the two sets. In a low, slow, gravelly voice, he said, "Come and get it, my sweet misbehavin' darlin'." With his fingers, he motioned for her to come toward him.

She smiled, he grinned back and moved backwards into the bedroom. When she was inside, he closed the doors and tossed the handcuffs onto the bed.

"Put these on."

"What if I don't?" She held them up for inspection. "I thought you said you weren't into kinky."

"Changed my mind." Carr shrugged.

"I like it that you can be flexible." She dropped the handcuffs on the bed. Then her hands were on his shirt, pushing it upward. He helped her, shrugging out of it, and slipped the straps of her dress from her shoulders, tugging it down. The disrobing was fast. Suddenly they were naked. After all they'd been through, the feel of her flesh against his, her breasts teasing his chest was nirvana to his soul.

"Lay on the bed." His command seemed to surprise her, her lips forming a perfect O. But she complied.

"What are you going to do?" she questioned, but she was on the bed and on her back seeming to sense what he wanted.

"It's a surprise." He picked up the handcuffs and taking one of her hands, he kissed the fingers then nipped and licked up her arm, watching her body respond. He put the handcuffs on her wrist and fastened the other pair to the bedpost. He did the same with her other arm and wrist.

"I'm going to erase the apprehension and the fear. You're going to think happy thoughts." He spread her legs, kissing her toes and the bottom of her feet. *Slow, go slow.*

"Carr, I want to touch you too." She tugged on the handcuffs, knew they would snap if she wanted them off.

"Later." He promised. "That's why you're handcuffed, so you can't touch me. I want you."

Working his way to the apex of her thighs, he kissed her, tasted her cream, working her clit with his tongue until he felt her buck and shudder against him. With his hands on her breasts, he tugged at the nipples. She cried out and more cream burst inside. Her flesh shimmered, an aura of silver surrounded her body and he wanted more, he needed everything, craved all of her.

He fumbled with the condom. "Hold on, sweetheart, I'll be inside you in a second. And he was. Hard and fast he drove inside, again and again. His lips searing her mouth and his tongue delving inside, tasting her, pulling on her lips, nipping then soothing them.

"Margo," he cried out her name, thrusting again and again until he was a mindless heap. Resting a moment, he kissed her nipple, licked and toyed with it then turned his attentions to her other silken nipple. He wanted this moment to last forever and he wanted her to touch him. Yet he knew he'd explode faster than ever if she ran her hands across his body.

He moved over and upward to where her wrists were shackled. Ripping the handcuff off with his teeth, he dropped it on her and moved to the other wrist. Her flesh simmered with silver rainbows.

"Orange flavor, yummy." She chewed on the candy.

Legs spread on either side of Margo, Carr ran his hands along her body, paying close attention to her breasts, then moving lower to run his hands across her flat belly wishing he felt his babe growing there.

He'd wanted to marry her before she became pregnant but now that they were wed, the decision was hers to make. He wanted children, lots of them.

"Want to give me more of that?" He looked at her wet pussy before grinning shamelessly.

"You exhaust me." She ran her hands through his hair and pulled him closer for another kiss.

"Is that a yes?"

She nodded, so he turned her over, kissing her tiny butt before pulling her to her knees.

"Oh my God, Carr."

He slipped inside, with his hands on her hips, he pulled her close and drove hard.

Again and again he drove until he felt her throb and pulse. She screamed out his name, her arms collapsing. Her spasms reached his soul and he climaxed with a primal cry of his own.

She lay panting on the bed, her sweat-sheened body still enticing him to touch and explore. God, but he never wanted to stop loving her.

"We've got to be quieter, Sophie," she whispered as she turned and let the weight of his body rest on hers.

"Yes..." he murmured then circled a soft nipple with his tongue. "Quiet, no noise. Don't say anything at all." His teeth closed on the nipple, tugging. Loved the way her hips rose to meet him, challenging him to pleasure her in so many new ways.

Her hands closed around his cock, her fingers working a magic that could not be denied. "Sweet misbehavin' darling, give me more of that," he rasped.

"Your command is my pleasure." She kissed her way down his torso, lingering on his abs, nipping across his flat belly. She licked the tip and circled him with her tongue before taking all of him inside her mouth. She sucked and played with him until he exploded inside her mouth.

"Fuck..."

He pulled her up so he could kiss her. Their tongues dueled for command, neither winning.

"Mama?"

The question was surreal and seemed to float on the silence.

Realization hit home with an impact that terrified. "Fuck." Margo reached for her a robe and found nothing.

Carr tossed her his shirt while he pulled on his pants. His heart raced harder than he ever thought possible.

"Mama?" Sophie stood in the doorway. "I thought I heard you scream."

"Oh, well, maybe." Margo put her arm around her little girl, and turned her around. "Everything is okay, honey. I'll take you back to bed and tuck you in again."

"I heard Carr scream too."

Carr stood beside the pair. "You did but it was a good scream. Someday I'll explain everything to you. Right now it's time to crawl back in bed and get a good night's sleep."

"You weren't hurting Mama were you? I won't like you if you did."

"I wouldn't like me either if I hurt her. And I promise you I never will do anything that harms your mother." Good Lord, the dynamics of making love with a little girl next door changed his life dramatically.

Sophie looked at him and smiled, and he knew that expression would always melt his heart.

"I'll just be a minute." Margo walked into Sophie's bedroom, her arm around the little girl's shoulder.

"Good, I'll wait out here." Suddenly struck with the sight of Margo clad in only his shirt, he hoped she'd go for that fashion more often.

He sat down, leaning back on the couch. They had so much to talk about. He had a hunch Phaedra was hoping they'd leave Tahoe, but he wasn't sure that was something Margo would want. Last night he'd stated they were leaving. The second the words were out of his mouth, he regretted them, but so much was happening, he hadn't talked to Margo. He put that discussion at the top of his list.

Going home to Cactus Junction and raising their children was good, damn good. He needed to show her where he grew up, the places he'd loved, Infinity Cliff, and he wanted to make love to her in the cave with the hot springs.

"Carr?" Margo sat down beside him.

"We need to be careful. I'm thinking our next home needs to have a separation of bedrooms." Wasn't that the truth, because he needed to hear Margo cry out his name and make those beautiful lovemaking sounds she did so well.

"Our next home? What do you have in mind, sexy man?" She ran her finger down the center of his chest.

"Will you come visit my home in the Sierra Madres?" He prayed she'd say yes and he wasn't sure what his next step would be if she told him no.

"I'd love to visit. Do you want to live there?" She toyed with the opening of his pants which he hadn't had time to fasten.

"Yes, but only if you do. It's just September. Would it be too difficult for Sophie to start in a new school?" He groaned, placing his hand on hers and moving her questing fingers away from his cock. He picked up her hand, kissing the palm. "Do you want to have Sophie walk in here and see us butt naked and me inside you."

She inhaled a sharp breath. "Of course not." Her voice turned icy and for a moment she looked away.

"What are you thinking?"

She nodded and pursed her lips. "That I'm three kinds a fool. I'll behave."

"Ah, but I like you misbehavin'. We just have to figure out how to find privacy when we have a six year old in the bedroom."

"When do you want to leave for Cactus Junction?"

Surprised, he said, "A couple of days. I'll have Brody send the jet back. Phaedra can move in and you can decide what you want to leave and what you want to take. I've furniture and a house of my own."

"You don't live with your parents?" she questioned. "For some reason, I thought you did live with them."

Someone tapped at the window. When Carr turned, he saw Brody peeking through the window. Margo must have realized it was Brody and raced to the bedroom. She came back with a floor length opaque robe draped around her.

Carr rushed to the door. "Fuck, is it morning? Come in. We haven't been asleep."

"I can see that. You might want to fasten your pants, or not. Here is the key." Brody handed him the card. "I'm leaving."

"Margo and I have decided to fly home in a couple of days. Will you send the jet to Tahoe?"

A grin spread across Brody's face. "Does that mean you're going to be livin' in Cactus Junction?"

"Maybe. Margo's decided to give the Sierra Madres a chance. I plan on convincing her it's the home she's never had."

"Got a little fixin' up of your place before you can live there," Brody said.

Carr shrugged. "That's where you come in, big bro. Can you convince Mom to help clean the old place up a little bit?"

"If you're bringing your bride home, it won't take any convincing. Mom will be in your house broom and duster in hand as soon as she hears the news."

Carr let out the breath he'd been holding. "Thanks. I'll see you in a few days then."

~ * ~

"Open your eyes." Holding his breath in anticipation, Carr slipped off the bandanna he'd put around Margo's eyes.

Speechless at the sight in front of her, she walked into the cave. The eerie darkness was relieved by a steady glow from mineral formations deep inside the cave.

At one of the walls, she reached out her hand to touch the bright sparkles of the light that shimmered in the back of the caves. "It's so beautiful. Oh! Is that a hot springs?" Margo moved closer, turning a three-sixty degree circle so she could take in all of the beauty.

"What do you think?" He grinned, wanting her to love this place as much as he did.

"Really Carr, I've never seen anything like this. The lights, they're magnificent and the steam rising from the water makes it all look surreal." She moved closer to the wall, reaching out her hands then turned her attention to the water, and bending down, she scooped up a handful. "So warm but not too hot, this will feel so good after the long ride."

"The temperature of the springs changes. In the winter it feels more like warm bath water than a hot tub."

"How? I thought hot springs were fed from underground."

He shrugged. "I don't know why. You can touch the lights but the wall will feel like plain old rock." Carr rocked back on his heels, grinning.

"Can we get in? Is it safe?" She wondered what it would be like to make love in water. The feel of liquid between their flesh seemed like pure sin.

"Only if you're naked." He pulled her into his arms, his hands slipping beneath her shirt.

She leaned back, closing her eyes, her head resting against his chest. "What about you?" She turned in his arms.

"Butt naked's the only way." He slipped her shirt over her head.

Margo winked at him. "I'll race you."

Scrambling to disrobe, Carr won. When she finished, he swept her into his arms and waded into the pool.

Heated water swirled around them. He settled a kiss on her lips, his hands roaming over her body, her breasts, her hips, her legs.

She had something damn important to talk to him about and she needed to do this before he swept her away sexually and mentally. "Carr stop."

"Hmm... don't want to stop." He nibbled kisses down her neck.

"Carr, really, I want to tell you something first." She was losing her ground and ready to succumb to his seduction and questing fingers.

"Please, this is important." She paused. "Oh my god, do that again."

It seemed he'd received her message. "Not until we talk." Looking into her eyes, a serious expression on his face, he pushed a lock of hair behind her ear. "What is it, sweet darlin'?"

Holding both of his hands, feeling vulnerable, she moistened her lips. "I've never told you this. I didn't even know how I felt at first because I was terrified. I had no idea where my life was headed and what part you would play." She looked away for a moment.

"And now you know?" He encouraged her.

"Yes," with a fingertip she touched his lips. "Carr, I love you."

For several seconds he didn't say anything. She was so afraid even though she shouldn't be. He'd told her countless times how much he loved her.

"I feel as if I've waited a lifetime to hear you say that and it's only been a few months since I met you. Margo, I love you so much I can't put it into words. You understand we are soul mates and we'll be together through eternity."

"I understand more now than when you first told me I was your mate."

He laughed. "That was a lot to take in at one time."

"I thought you were crazy."

"Ah, but now that you've confessed your love, I have something else we need to talk about."

She wasn't sure what else there was to say. "What?" she asked cautiously.

"How do you feel about kids?"

"We talked about children, I'd love more but we've plenty of time to start a family."

He lifted her chin. "No, we don't."

"What are you talking about?"

He kissed her then pulled her into his arms for a deeper one. She reveled in the feelings sweeping within, and heat radiating in every part of her.

Once again, he pulled away and lifted her chin so she could see into his eyes. "You, my sweet misbehavin' darlin', are pregnant."

"Don't joke."

"I'm not. Remember a week ago when we made love in Gramp's shower?"

"Go on."

"A, well, we forgot the condom."

"That was only a week. I don't even know."

"But shifters can touch their mate's belly and know. I felt your child inside you yesterday."

Stunned didn't come close to what she felt, a child. Was she ready and what would she tell Sophie?

"Margo, tell me what you're thinking. Are you happy?" His hands rested on her shoulders.

Tears slipped down her cheeks and he wiped one away. "Yes, yes, I'm happy."

She pulled Car into her arms. "Make love to me."

"Oh darling, you don't have to ask me twice."

"Carr, I love you."

"I love you too."

About the Author

achristay@aol.com

Born in Medford, Oregon, novelist Christine Young has lived in Oregon all of her life. After graduating from Oregon State University with a BS in science, she spent another year at Southern Oregon State University working on her teaching certificate, and a few years later received her Master's degree in secondary education and counseling. Now the long, hot days of summer provide the perfect setting for creating romance. She sold her first book, Dakota's Bride, the summer of 1998 and her second book, My Angel to Kensington. Her teaching and writing careers have intertwined with raising three children. Christine's newest venture is the creation of Rogue Phoenix Press. Christine is the founder, editor and co-owner with her husband. They live in Salem, Oregon.

Other books by Christine Young
Available at Rogue Phoenix Press

Catching Meara
The first book in the McKenna Clan Series

Meara Thorton was a feisty, world-class computer hacker—cornered by the FBI and shockingly given the chance to be their newly acquired technical analyst. Brilliant and intuitive, yet aching with the loss of everyone she has cared about, her restless heart led her to discover a love she fought and a world she didn't know could possibly exist.

Jace McKenna was an enigma, a loner, impossibly handsome, sincere and committed. The Apache shapeshifter blood running through his veins burned hotter than the blistering Sierra Madre sun. Jace knew the moment he caught Meara's scent she was his for eternity.

Sweet Sexy Sadie
The second book in the McKenna Clan Series

From the first time Sadie's eyes met those of Brody McKenna in the hot Sierra Madre Mountains, theirs was a potent attraction—not gentle, slow, and easy, but hot, hard, and all-consuming. The daughter of a dysfunctional family, Sadie had dreams no man could wrench from her with hot sex and an all-consuming passion. She'd challenge this alpha male with all the strength she possessed. But her red hair, fiery temperament, and indomitable spirit obsessed Brody...and he knew he had to find a way to show her he was more than he appeared and convince her to make a life with him.

Highland Honor
The first book in the Highland Series

Willfully stubborn, innocently courageous, Callie Whitcomb braves a journey through the treacherous highlands to the Macpherson castle. Callie flees from an unwanted marriage as well as her ruthless half brother. Naively she believes Colin MacPherson, the head of the clan, is loyal to her father and will give her sanctuary, protecting her from the vile plans that have been made for her.

As hard and as unyielding as the winter storms that sweep through the countryside, Colin is irresistibly drawn to the impetuous beauty who has magically appeared on his doorsteps. Despite his vows of revenge against her father, she stirs his passion as well as his sense of justice...but to love her would violate all his vows of revenge.

Highland Magic
The second book in the Highland Series

Throughout the Highlands she is known as Keely, the witch woman. She is a great healer-a woman whose dreams come true. Ian MacPherson is a man who puts honor, loyalty and duty above everything. Their lives are entwined when Ian is sent by the Scottish King to bring Keely to trial for witchcraft. He is attacked and left for dead, but Keely rescues him. When he wakes, he discovers he has no memory. As he remembers his lost past, Ian finds that his need to protect the woman who has saved his life eclipses his duty to his king and country., He is a man torn between honor and duty to his country and the woman he loves.

Highland Song
The third book in the Highland Series

With her white-gold hair and azure eyes, Lainie MacPherson is as wild and untamed as the rugged Scottish Highlands where she was raised. Lainie vowed to avenge her rape. Recklessly, she defies English laws and the man who raped her puts a bounty on her head. The man who is sent to bring her to Edinburgh sets a dangerous trap. With nothing left to live for the beautiful Scottish spy steals the sealed documents the English soldier has tempted her with.

When the exquisite temptress takes the bait and runs off with not only the forged documents but the purses of the men in the tavern, Aaron Slade vows to hunt her down and bring her to justice, never dreaming she will tame his jaded soul. When Aaron discovers the truth about the tempestuous woman who stirs his passion to the point of madness, he dares not love her, but desires her with all his soul.

Dakota's Bride
The first book in the Lakota/Pinkerton Series

When Emma St. John received her brother's letter imploring her to escape her stepfather's vengeful scheme and to trust Dakota Barringer with her life, she was willing to chance it. But the handsome, brooding riverboat owner Emma found in Natchez a danger of another kind. For Emma soon found herself surrendering to an unrelenting desire.

Raised by the Sioux when his parents were killed, Dakota had been betrayed once before by a white woman. He wasn't about to trust another, especially one claiming that her stepfather, a powerful U.S. senator, had framed her as a murderess. But he couldn't let Emma's intoxicating effect on him. Now Dakota would risk his very life to protect the innocent beauty who had seduced him with her tender love.

My Angel

The second book in the Lakota/Pinkerton Series

A BEAUTY IN BUCKSKINS

When her father decided to send her to a finishing school back East, Angela Chamberlain refused to be confined to stuffy drawing rooms. Instead, the daring spitfire who could shoot like a man and ride like the wind longed for a life of adventure and romance—and she knew exactly who could give it to her. Devil Blackmoor was a hired gun with a dangerous reputation. But Angela was willing to go to the ends of the earth to capture the handsome devil's heart.

A DEVIL IN DISGUISE

He'd come to America looking for excitement, but Devil Blackmoor got more than he bargained for when he encountered a beautiful rebel who answered his kisses with a wild innocence that touched his very soul. Yet standing between them were more obstacles than either ever dreamed. For Devil had strapped on a gun for the wrong man. And that made Angela his enemy. Now he'll have to choose between his duty and the woman he loves more than life.

The Locket

The third book in the Lakota/Pinkerton Series

The year is 1894. Seeking revenge for crimes against his family, Misha Petrovich follows a path that leads straight to Ariel Cameron's boarding house in Mist Harbor, Oregon. A family heirloom in Ariel's possession leads Misha to believe she is guilty. The locket has been handed down to the oldest girl in the Petrovich family for generations.

Ariel is innocent of wrong doing, but her father is not. Misha is torn by his feelings for Ariel and his need for restitution against her father. Knowing that the relationship between them is fragile, Misha does everything in his power to protect Ariel's father. His efforts are to no avail when her father is shot. Ariel comes to realize Misha's steadfast courage and determination to protect her and her father despite what has happened to his family. Ariel's love and devotion heals Misha's heart.

The Talisman

The fourth book in the Lakota/Pinkerton Series

Running from a marriage that lasted one night, Dr. Moriah McKeown discovers the land she has settled on is coveted by determined and lawless men. Yet the proud young woman who once vowed never to abandon her home has second thoughts when her adopted children are threatened. Her only recourse is to enlist the aid of a dark, dangerous gun for hire.

Haunted by the past and a betrayal he will never forgive, Ian Civanovich uses his fast gun and his reckless courage to forget the faithlessness of a woman in his past. He will trust no female--nor will he rest until the threat hovering over Moriah McKeown is put to rest.

Forever His

The fifth book in the Lakota/Pinkerton Series

Struggling to come to terms with the part she played in Jacob St. John's death, Etta Barringer resigns from Pinkerton Agency and seeks peace and solace in a Rocky Mountain Cabin.

Jacob has vowed to discover the reason Etta has betrayed him, sold him out to his enemy and left him for dead.

Isolated in their cabin, they discover their love for each other and learn to trust. But the trust is shattered when Jacob learns she is married to his sworn enemy; the man who left him in the desert to die.

Allura

The first book in the Twelve Dancing Princesses Series

Allura McClellan is horrified by her father's decision to take out an ad in the Times awarding her to the man strong enough and smart enough to win her hand and uncover her secrets. She's an intelligent young woman who takes great delight in the freedom allotted to her by her father. She's well aware that marriage would effectively curtail the adventures she's shared with her sisters and cousins.

Hunter Gray is nothing like the other men who've arrived to vie for Allura's hand in marriage and everything that goes along with it. However, he is the first to refuse to concede defeat and pursue her despite her attempts to disguise her true appearance. It's her temperament that is of more concern to him than her looks. Hunter has worked all his life with the hope of someday owning his own land. Now that it looks like there's a very real possibility that everything he's ever wanted is within reach nothing is going to deter him – including Miss Allura's disagreeable disposition.

The Wager

The second book in the Twelve Dancing Princesses Series

Amorica Hepburn was sent to London to find a husband. Finding a man was the last item on her agenda. With her two cousins, Amorica wagers she can dissuade her suitor before the others. Despite her efforts she discovers a chemistry that cannot be denied. Suddenly she is the arrogant man's wife, pledged to a marriage neither desire. But swept off to his ancestral home above the Dover cliffs and into his strong embrace, Amorica is soon possessed by a raging passion for the husband she had vowed to despise…

Damian Andrews couldn't afford to trust the emerald-eyed spitfire who happened upon his secret. Amorica's hatred of all men of his kind only inflames the war that rages between them. Still, he can not control the intense desire his stubborn bride inspires, or make her surrender to his will until he has conquered the headstrong beauty on the battlefield of love…

A Marriage of Inconvenience
The third book in the Twelve Dancing Princesses Series

A REGAL BEAUTY

When the duchess decides to wed her to a wastrel and a fop, Ravyn Grahm takes matters into her own hands and declares her engagement to another man. Instead of fessing up and telling her great aunt what she has done, she goes through with the pretense. Aric Lakeland is the bastard son of an earl and has a dangerous reputation. But Ravyn is willing to do most anything to keep the duchess from discovering the lie.

A DEVIL-MAY-CARE SMUGGLER

He'd bought land in America, looking to put down roots and end his life of adventure, but Aric Lakeland got more than he bargained for when he encountered a beautiful heiress who made a promise she didn't want to keep. But the promise could not be undone and standing between them were more obstacles than either ever dreamed. Aric had made plans to spend the rest of his life in America and that was at odds with Ravyn's plan of living in England and running her father's estate. Now, he'll have to choose between his dreams and the woman he loves more than life.

Rebel Heart

HER REBEL SPIRIT DEFIED HIS OUTSIDERS SOUL...
She was velvet and silk, eyes the color of a summer storm and amber hair. Victoria DeMontville, because of a promise and a codicil to her father's will, was forced to marry one man to protect her from another. She hated Cameron Savage with a fierce passion. But to hold on to her genetic research and find a cure for the deadly Signe virus, she must pretend to love the enemy at her door, come with weapons of fire to melt her icy heart...

HIS OUTSIDERS TOUCH IGNITED RAGING PASSIONS...
He wore a mask, disguised as the Phantom, a true legend come to life. Even as war and debate over new genetic research engulfed them all, he would find his greatest adversary in the beauty who'd branded him an outsider and barbarian, the woman he was born to possess, his soul mate.

A St. Patrick's Day Tale

by

Christine Young, C. L. Kraemer, Genene Valleau

Tumble through time…

…to Ireland in 1817, when tensions are high between Protestants and Chatolics and faey people guide the fate of villagers. A lovely Catholic lass stumbles upon the weakly ritual fisticuffing between Irish lads. She falls into the lap of a handsome young Protestant. Family ties, grudges, and two conniving faeries threaten their budding love. But the faeries outsmart themselves when they hijack a time machine that has mysteriously appeared in their forest and are whisked to…

...Eugene, Oregon in the 20th century, amid a property feud between the local faeries and night elves. The conniving faeries from Olde Ireland try to stir up more mischief. However, a warrior gnome convinces the magic folk to control their own destiny, and forces the intruding faeries to take refuge in the time machine again, spinning their way toward...

...A modern day castle in western Oregon. An eccentric inventor is determined to reclaim his wayward time machine and save his beloved wife from her latest misadventure. If only they can travel safely past the black hole...

A Valentine's Anthology

The Lending Library-a fantasy by Christie L. Kraemer

Faeries try to fit into the human world when the forest where they make their home is destroyed by a mysterious enemy.

Chasing Rainbows-a contemporary romance by Genene Valleau

An eccentric aunt, an inventive uncle, a mother who wears poodle skirts, and a brother who wears pearls provide a hilarious backdrop for the courtship of a young woman who yearns for a "normal" family.

The Gift-an historical romance by Christine Young

A man and a woman on opposite sides of the Civil War get a second chance at love after one final battle returns soldiers to their war-torn homes to rebuild their lives.

Writing as AnnChristine
Safari Moon

Solo St. John, a wildlife photographer, is preparing for a trip to Alaska. Suddenly, Solo finds women of all sorts invading his privacy, his home and his office, all cooing nonsense words and blatantly throwing themselves at him. Solo doesn't know why, and he has no idea how to rid himself of the persistent women. He finally decides to beg a favor of his best buddy Nyssa Harrington.

In love with Solo for the past ten years and knowing he doesn't return her feelings Nyssa doesn't want to talk to Solo. She knows if she accepts his phone call, she will not be able to resist the temptation to hope again.

A Valentine's Anthology

Sharks
byAnnChristine

Will Lily and Jacob, best friends forever, find love or will they discover friendship is not enough for a relationship to take the final step into marriage.

The House on Berkley Street
by K. J. Dahlen

When Serenity is asked to find the truth in a forty-year old tragedy, someone in the town of White Oak, Texas doesn't want the truth told. Can they stop her before she finds out what they have kept hidden for so long?

The Placebo Effect
by Solstice Stevens

First, there was the poison. Then, there was a four story jump and the basketball hoop. Jessamyn Hamhill's life has been one validation attempt after another . . . until now.

www.ingramcontent.com/pod-product-compliance
Lightning Source LLC
Chambersburg PA
CBHW060219180626
46813CB00007B/2883

9781624202599